DITCH LANE DIARIES:
RUBY'S CHOICE

D. F. JONES

RUBY'S CHOICE
Copyright © 2014, D.F. Jones, all rights reserved.
ISBN: 978-0-9861227-4-3 paperback
ISBN: 978-0-9861227-3-6 ebook

Notes:
No part of this book may be reproduced in any form, including, but not limited to, any electronic forms, and information or storage systems without the explicit written permission from the author.

This is a work of fiction. Names, characters, places and incidents are either the products of the author's imagination or are used fictitiously, and any resemblance to actual persons, living or dead, business establishments, events or locales is completely coincidental.

Cover design by Jones Media art director Amanda Northcutt. Photo of the image is leased through Istock.com
Interior formatting by Author E.M.S.

Published in the United States of America.

To my wonderful husband and best friend, KJ

Acknowledgments

I am forever in debt to those family and friends who have supported my endeavor to write *Ruby's Choice*. My husband, for enduring my endless obsession with writing *Ruby's Choice*, the first book of the Ditch Lane Diaries series. He has always supported and encouraged me. My sons, for always showing their mom love and respect while offering their encouragement and input. Thank you to my parents. My dad has always been the consummate storyteller. My mom has always been my biggest cheerleader and a hopeless romantic.

Thank you to my bestie, Denise. She has been my sounding board from the inception of this project. She offered ideas, suggestions and was one of the first to read *Ruby's Choice*. Thank you to all of my Beta Readers: Erin, Doris, Sherrie, Bettina, Debby, your comments and insights were so valuable to me.

I want to express my sincere appreciation and gratitude to my editor, Emme Adams. She rocks! She took on my project and worked diligently to help me find my voice. I have grown as a writer because of her patience and efforts. Her guidance and insight continue to be invaluable to me.

I would like to give a huge shout out to Amanda, my creative director. She designed the book cover and my marketing materials. She is absolutely wonderful at making my projects look great! Thanks to Tiffany for the initial copy editing.

And lastly, to my readers: Thank you for following my updates on social media! You were all so positive, encouraging and patient during my writing journey. This book is for you! I trust you will love *Ruby's Choice* and follow me with the upcoming books in the Ditch Lane Diaries.

Fun Fact: Chapter Titles Are Songs from the 1970's enjoy!

Contents

	Prologue	1
1	Dream Weaver	5
2	Hot Fun in the Summertime	21
3	Knock It Out of the Park	39
4	Stuck in the Middle with You	53
5	Rock the Boat	63
6	If I Were Your Woman	79
7	Take It to the Limit	89
8	Strange Magic	101
9	Tonight's the Night	107
10	Boogie Nights	127
11	Get Away	137
12	Oh Girl	147
13	Show Me the Way	161
14	Dancing in the Moonlight	165
Epilogue	Simple Twist of Fate	171

Prologue

Campbell Ridge Cave 1972

Ruby, Anna and Sandy had their backpacks filled with water, extra flashlights and batteries for spelunking the cave on Campbell Ridge. Ruby had discovered the entrance of the cave with her brother, George, five years ago, when they were looking for Indian arrowheads. George had told her never under any circumstances to go inside of the cave. But today, Ruby and her best friends, Anna and Sandy, were looking for new adventures.

The girls were deep inside the cave, surrounded by complete darkness with only their flashlights to illuminate the interior walls. The limestone cave had beautiful rock formations, crystals and stalactites. The cave underground had seemed alien, almost unworldly. The air smelled of the dank earth, and the only sound was running water from the stream that ran through the cave.

Ruby was forced to climb over a boulder on her belly to squeeze through a narrow pass. The boulder opened up into a hidden room. Ruby was still hanging onto the rock when she yelled back at the girls, "Hey, guys, you have to see this!" And then she slid down the rock into the room.

Anna and Sandy scrambled up and over the boulder, shining their lights into the hidden room. Anna slid down the boulder and entered with Sandy right behind her. The hidden room was roughly the size of a bedroom. "Holy cow, there are ancient drawing's on the wall."

Thousands of years of groundwater had caused the rocks on one side of the cave to drop down forming large stalactites the size of a pickup truck. The large drawings revealed intricate details of each person etched in the stone wall. Sandy inspected the drawings closer as she walked down the length of the wall. "It's a story. I read about ancient drawings like these in one of my *National Geographic* magazines. This is far out."

Ruby tripped over a small rock, dropping her flashlight. The light on the ground lit the far left corner, revealing a massive figure carved in the stone. "Geez Louise! This dude looks like a freaking astronaut. Look at his helmet!"

Anna bumped into Ruby, nearly making them both fall down. She held onto Ruby's shoulder and said, "That's some spooky shit."

Anna walked past Sandy to the next group of drawings. "Here's the same dude again. He's holding a totem and there are three people kneeling before him. This looks like a ritual or rite of passage."

Sandy sat down on a rock, mesmerized by what they had discovered. She flashed her light toward Ruby and Anna as they traced their fingers over the different drawings. Sandy asked, "Do you think we should tell our parents or teachers?"

Anna and Ruby walked over sit to on the ground next to Sandy. Ruby's light fused with Sandy's as Anna's light circled around to the other parts of the room. There was only one wall dedicated to the drawings. Anna replied, "I don't think so. A tribe sealed this room for some reason. We should leave. I've got a weird feeling, like we're being watched."

Sandy stood, tipping over the rock she had been sitting on, causing her flashlight to point downward. "Hey, look, something's under this rock. Bring your lights over here." Anna and Sandy shined their lights over the place where the rock had been, as Ruby knelt down, reached in and pulled out the object.

The girls plopped back down on the hard ground, staring wide-eyed at the totem. Ruby's voice trembled. "It's the totem in the drawing, the same one the deity is handing over to the people kneeling on the ground. I know this sounds weird, but this thing is pulsing in my hands."

Sandy reached over to pluck the totem out of Ruby's hand. The totem was around six inches tall, made out of crystal and quartz with piercing sapphire eyes. The detailed carvings made the image of the face appear real, smooth as glass to the touch, as though sculpted by a master artisan, and no matter which way they turned the totem, it seemed to be watching them. "It's a smaller version of the big guy in the corner. He is looking at me."

Sandy handed the totem to Anna, who turned it over in her hands. "I see what you mean. This little dude is shooting energy to my fingertips. We need to place this thing back where we found it and get the hell out of Dodge. I have the creeps in here."

Ruby took the totem and put it back in the hole. In another part of the cave, Ruby could hear rocks falling. "We need to get out of here because the cave is shifting." The girls rolled the boulder back in place and made a hasty exit.

Outside in the daylight, they sat on a rock ledge, out of breath and speechless. Ruby opened her backpack and pulled out an amber-encased spider web. "Well, shut the front door, what the heck? Look y'all, it's a spider web inside a piece of amber?"

Anna found an amethyst stone in her pocket, and Sandy opened her thermos finding a hiddenite stone. Anna shook her head in bewilderment. "Well, I'm pretty sure these stones weren't with us before we went inside the cave. If I wasn't so dad blame scared, I'd take this back inside the cave, right now."

Sandy stared at her stone and then spoke quietly. "I don't want to spook you any further, but holding this stone gave me a vision of the deity who gave us the stones. In the vision, he is relaying that we're to keep the stones on our person at all times. He will reveal to us in time what it means and we aren't supposed to talk about this again until he reveals it to Ruby in a dream."

The girls looked at each other wide-eyed, holding their stones in eerie silence. They never uttered a single word about the totem or the stones again—until years later.

Chapter 1

Dream Weaver

*Everglade, Tennessee
Summer 1977*

RUBY STOCKED THE SHELVES FOR tomorrow's store traffic. Summer always brought in an influx of tourists, along with the store regulars. Her workday was coming to a close, which meant it was time to party. As she stacked the last rows of Dove soap and Jergens body lotion, she began to daydream. She bit back a playful smile, recalling the delicious dream from the night before.

In Ruby's dream, she walked hand-in-hand with a stranger down a long sidewalk lined with pink dogwood trees in full bloom. The sun shone brightly as she looked up at him. She raised her hand, framing her eyes to deflect the sun so she could see his face more clearly. Her dream man turned and looked down at her with kind, expressive eyes and laughed. Ruby felt love; it surrounded and embraced her.

The dream shifted as she followed him into a bedroom. The wall-to-wall bay window in the room overlooked the night lights of a city. Ruby stood only inches from him, not touching, but just looking into his eyes.

The dream shifted again. The man had disappeared and Ruby turned around frantically looking for him. She found him sitting on the edge of the bed. Ruby trembled as she walked toward him. He reached for her.

The edges of her dream blurred as purple, yellow and blue hues distorted in her vision, and he seemed to shimmer away. Ruby tried hard to zero in on his face, and then he reappeared, clear and in focus. She sat down beside him, and he reached up to run his finger across her bottom lip. He cradled her face with his hand, and then he leaned down slowly covering her mouth with his, as she circled her arms around his neck. His kiss was so soft and tender that it sent a wave of pleasure washing over her so acute her mind seemed to go blank. Ruby felt him smile against her lips, and then he pulled back slightly and adjusted his angle so he could nibble on her earlobe, sending shivers up her spine.

Ruby ran her fingers over his shoulders and down his well-defined biceps, as she arched toward him. Every nerve ending in her sizzled, and she cried out to him, "I love you." Red-hot sensations spread through her like wildfire in a parched forest.

Ruby lay back on the bed, and his body rose over hers and then he pressed his face so close to hers, his lips barely brushed against her cheek. Mr. Dreamy traced his finger down her jawline and whispered, "I'm on fire for you and now you're mine."

Snap out of it! Ruby quickly recovered from her daydreaming as she heard her boss call her name.

Mr. Burns asked, "Ruby, honey, would you work the cash register for me so I can work on my books?"

Ruby replied politely, "Yes, sir, Mr. Burns."

Mr. Burns had been teaching Ruby the art of running a small business since she was sixteen. She dreamed of owning her own grocery store, some day, and she had saved nearly five hundred dollars to use for start-up capital. She had a five-year plan from the time she graduated college in two years to the time she would open her doors.

Everglade General Store had been in the Burns family for forty years. The wooden exterior of the old-fashioned store had been painted white, and the interior walls revealed exposed logs and wood beams. The store had been renovated several years ago, but Mr. Burns had purposely kept the interior the same to reflect the era when his father had built it in 1938. Several huge wicker ceiling fans hung overhead, and the checkout counter still had glass-encased bins for candy and treats.

Ruby took off her apron and was making her way behind the

counter when she saw the front door open and two guys stroll into the store. She was checking the guys out when the one on the left looked up and caught her staring.

Holy smokes! It's the guy in my dream!

It always blew Ruby away whenever something from her dreams appeared in real life. Ever since she had found the piece of amber that day in the cave with Sandy and Anna, she'd had life-or-death dreams, and occasionally she would see glimpses into the future. Typically, her life dreams would foretell the birth of a child for a friend or relative, and then she would find out days after her dream, a friend or relative was pregnant.

Ruby's worst dreams were the ones about death. She hated those dreams. The first one had been about her Aunt Sammie. In Ruby's dream, her aunt had been driving down the interstate and tried to miss debris from a jackknifed tractor-trailer. Her car had slammed into the guardrail. The dream shifted to the emergency room, where the family had decided not to continue life support. Thirty minutes after Ruby had woken from that awful dream she had received a phone call and learned her aunt had been in a terrible car accident. Ruby learned her aunt had indeed hit a tractor-trailer, but in reality the truck had crossed into her traffic lane. Ruby had rushed to the hospital, where the scene in the ER had unfolded just like the latter part of her dream—the family had pulled her aunt's life support. To this day, Ruby hated having death dreams, but thankfully, they were few and far between.

Occasionally, she would have a dream like the one she'd had last night that involved people she had never met before. The guy in her dream last night apparently was real. Watching her real-life dream man walk into the store sent chills straight up her arms.

Ruby locked on his beautiful dark eyes, the color of espresso and framed with thick, luscious lashes. A fireball ripped through her as she ogled the dark-haired, warrior-like god who stood at least six feet tall. She could see his rippling muscles bursting through his tight, white T-shirt, which starkly contrasted with his suntan. He smiled at her with dazzling white teeth, and Ruby's knees literally went weak.

For crying out loud, she was acting like a lovesick fool, fidgeting back and forth, trying not to look directly at the guy. Dreamy's head lifted and his eyes locked on hers again, sucking her in. She felt an instantaneous spark, a strange sort of electricity radiating from him to her. Only a moment had passed before she looked away, embarrassed for being caught gawking at him like he was a hot piece of Southern pecan pie and she hadn't eaten for a month.

And then, Ruby noticed the second guy. He had the most striking green eyes, jet-black hair, and lips that made her want to kiss them. She just didn't see gorgeous guys like these two every day in Everglade.

They were whispering to each other and chuckling as they walked past the counter. Ruby knew the blood must be rushing to her face. The two guys walked with such confidence, and they were so self-assured. Her gaze followed them to the refrigerated section in the back of the store. She watched them grab two Sundrop sodas and then head toward the candy aisle. When the guys walked toward the check-out, Ruby started straightening the items on the counter, trying to look busy. On the surface, she maintained a cool demeanor, but on the inside her nerves were bouncing off the walls.

REED HAD DRIVEN OUT TO Everglade with Brent to check out the hot sister of George Glenn, the manager of their summer baseball team. George had invited Reed and Brent to a party tonight at Ditch Lane, a local hangout for college students. Since the season started, the guys on their baseball team had been talking about George's little sister, and those who had been brave enough to ask her out had been shot down. Reed had always loved a challenge, though.

Reed whispered to Brent, "*Tap It*! That little honey is going to be mine."

Brent chuckled, as he tried to push Reed out of the way for a better look at the girl behind the counter. "No way, dude. The game is on."

Reed and Brent had always competed against each other—from sports to women. Because they were always chasing the same women, during their freshman year at Middle Tennessee State University, they came up with a game called *Tap It*. In *Tap It*, they would choose one girl, and then they both dated her until she professed her undying love for either Brent or Reed. The winner of the game would get to date the girl exclusively while the loser had to pay the other one's bar tab for a month.

Reed and Brent walked to the front of the store and placed their sodas and candy on the counter. Reed hooked his thumbs in his blue-jean pockets as Brent rested his hand on top of the cash register. Both of the guys were checking out every inch of George's little sister's body.

RUBY STRAIGHTENED HER SPINE, LIFTED her chin, looked Dreamy straight in his eyes, and flashed him a Colgate Ultra Brite smile. "Will that be all for you today?"

Mr. Dreamy said, "Yes, ma'am. This is it. Y'all been busy today?" His voice had a sweet Southern drawl.

Ruby began ringing up their items on the cash register. "Yes, Fridays and Saturdays are the worst." She tossed a glance over her shoulder to make sure Mr. Burns hadn't heard her.

Green Eyes turned to see who she was looking at and then turned back to her and winked. "You're safe; he's not looking." He paused slightly and then said, "Hey, we're looking for Ditch Lane. George Glenn invited us to a party there tonight. Would you mind giving me directions?"

Ruby placed their items in a brown paper bag. Her head shot up when she heard the bells chime from the store door opening again, and more people came in. *Crap, it's time to close. Don't people ever read the hours on the front door?* She looked back to the guys at the counter. "That'll be sixty-five cents." She paused and then said, "George Glenn? He's my brother."

Dreamy placed sixty-five cents on the counter and leaned in a little too close. "I didn't realize George had such a pretty sister. I'm Reed Jackson, and this is my friend, Brent Brown."

Ruby picked up the money and opened the register drawer, dropping the coins in their specified slots, and said casually, "Nice to meet you. I'm Ruby."

Reed pulled his drink out of the bag and popped the top. "Well, hello, Ruby. I like your name. It's a good ole Southern name."

Good ole Southern name...is he joking? She smiled inwardly—surely he had a better pickup line. Ruby's name had been in the Glenn family tree for generations.

Brent reached for the bag and pulled out his drink and Snickers bar. He handed the empty bag back to Ruby. "We're playing on your brother's baseball team this summer. Do you ever come out and watch him play?"

Ruby noticed the other customers in the store were nearly finished shopping, and then she returned her attention to Brent. "I haven't seen him play this year, but I'll make it to one of his baseball games before the season ends."

George had formed an adult men's baseball team to compete in the Williamson County League in Franklin. He looked for talent around the Middle Tennessee area to play on his team. She wondered where George had found these two. Ruby planned on getting the scoop on Reed and Brent tomorrow when she went swimming with George's wife, Lizzie.

Ruby watched Reed as he turned his head around to check out the other shoppers in the store. There was a little boy who was running up and down the aisle with a toy wind fan, and his mother was shouting to the boy to put it back. The little boy was screeching, refusing to let go of the toy.

Reed shook his head and turned his attention back to her. Reed's gaze flickered to her lips and then rose back up to her eyes, which made her nervously shift her feet. Her palms began to sweat.

Reed lifted a brow and then asked, "So, are you going to the party tonight?"

Ruby sat back on the little stool behind the counter and crossed her arms. Her knee was unconsciously bouncing up and down. She tried to exude a laid-back attitude, but her blood thundered through her veins. "Yeah, I'm meeting some friends there later."

Reed placed his arm on the glass bin, leaned closer and asked, with a sly and very sexy sideways grin, "Are they 'girl' friends or 'guy' friends?"

Ruby arched her brow and leaned closer to him. "Both."

Brent and Reed both laughed loudly at Ruby's comeback. Brent slapped Reed on the back and said, "She's got your number, brother." Reed shrugged his right shoulder and took a step back.

Little Tommy, the kid who had been running in the aisle, was throwing a huge temper tantrum now as his mother physically removed the toy from his fingers. Mr. Burns walked out of his office to go talk with the boy's mother. He rustled the hair on the boy's head and Ruby overheard Mr. Burns tell Tommy's mom the boy could have the toy.

Ruby's eyes were drawn back to Brent. He straightened his shoulders and flexed his chest muscles, as he rubbed his hand down his bicep. *Dang, that boy is off the charts!*

Brent placed his arm on the register. "So, what time are you going?"

"I have to close tonight, so probably in an hour or so. Why?"

Brent stepped around the counter and whispered in her ear, "So, I can kiss you."

Reed shook his head, laughing under his breath. Brent stepped back and shoved his hands in his pockets. He looked so cool—like he expected her to fall at his feet or something.

Ruby's face flushed, but she remained in control and brushed off his advance. The lady and her son were walking toward the front of the store now. She jumped off the stool. "Oh, you need directions. Ditch Lane isn't far from here. Take a right when you pull out of the store's parking lot onto Highway 99, and then take your first right onto Concord Road. Follow the road for about three miles."

Reed raised a hand to interrupt her. "Hold on a minute. Do you have a pencil so I can write this down on my paper bag?" Ruby reached into the drawer under the counter and handed him a pencil. Reed began to write down what she had just told them and then said, "Okay, I've got it. What's after the three miles?" He poised the pencil in his hand to continue writing.

Ruby slowed down her directions so Reed could keep up. "You'll come to a huge curve that bears to the right—take the street on the left. That's Taylor Road. You'll drive about three more miles, and then you'll see an old white plantation house on the left. Ditch Lane is on the left before the house's driveway. You'll see the cars."

Reed finished writing the directions down and then read them back to Ruby to verify he had them correct. His smile broadened. "Cool. Thanks for the directions, and if we don't see you tonight, I'll be looking for you at one of the games."

Ruby's hand rested on top of the cash register. Brent gently picked up her hand and rubbed his thumb across the top. "I'll be looking for you, sweet girl."

She stared at Brent but didn't reply as she nervously bit her bottom lip. She had been unconsciously holding her breath. When they walked out the door, she let out a sigh. Ruby turned her attention to ringing up the last customers of the day.

Did that just really happen? Those two guys are smoking hot!

Ruby walked over to Mr. Burns. "Is it okay to place the closed sign on the door and close out the register?"

He looked up and scratched his head. Mr. Burns walked over to the cash register. "Sure Ruby. I'll get the register and close out. You're off tomorrow, but I have you scheduled to work next week on Tuesday, Wednesday, and Friday, two o'clock to eight."

"Yes, sir. I have marked it on my calendar. Then it's okay for me to leave?"

Mr. Burns rubbed his lower back and then tapped her shoulder. "Yes, honey, go have fun, but *be safe*."

RUBY DROVE DOWN THE BACK roads of Everglade. She had her radio blasting while she howled at the full moon. Thirty minutes later she arrived at Ditch Lane. She parked her car and headed out to find her friends and the two hunks from the store.

Ditch Lane was a dead-end road where a small bridge had been washed out from years of flooding from the creek. During this time of the year, the creek at the end of the lane was not deep enough to swim in, but on a hot summer night it was nice to sit on the bank and let your feet dangle in the water while you partied with your friends. Laughter echoed throughout the hollow, and tunes from the Steve Miller Band's "Fly like an Eagle" had been cranked up on *someone's* car radio. *Ruby* walked through what seemed to be fifty people, stopping to chat for a second or two with old high school friends, before seeing Anna and Sandy sitting on a log next to the bonfire.

"Hey, girlie, where have you been?" Sandy asked. She had been talking to Rusty Sanders, an old high school flame.

"This girl has to work for a living. Guess what?" Ruby said, and continued on without a pause, "Mr. Burns has decided to allow me to negotiate with two of the major food reps for the store. I'm so excited!"

Anna gave her a hug. "Ruby, that's rocks!"

Ruby gave them both high fives. "Yeah, I know I'm pretty psyched about the whole thing." She took a step closer to Sandy and Anna and then whispered in a low voice so no one else could hear her, "By any chance have y'all seen two gorgeous guys out here looking for my brother?"

Sandy grabbed a brew from the cooler next to Rusty's truck and walked with Ruby and Anna to the creek. "Hot dang! They were here with George. I haven't seen Grade A choice meat like that in a long time." Sandy fanned herself like she had the vapors and then tipped the can to her lips and took a long drink of her beer.

The girls sat down by the creek, took off their sandals and placed their feet in the water. The full moon shone through the trees as a gentle warm breeze caressed them. The smell of honeysuckle and a symphony of crickets filled the summer air.

Anna's eyes widened and then she looked around to make sure no one had followed them. "Reed and Brent were here. They left because George had to take Lizzie home. She wasn't feeling very well." Ruby lay down on the ground and looked up at the stars. Anna turned around to face her and sat cross-legged while Sandy continued to splash her feet in the water.

Anna looked as though she was getting ready to reveal a big secret. "I met Reed and Brent last semester at a frat party. Girl, that Brent is too hot to handle, and I've never seen him date the same girl more than a few times. And Reed is such a hunk! He's from East Tennessee but lives in Murfreesboro. He's a senior at MTSU. I think he may have a girlfriend."

Ruby rose up with a frown. "Reed has a girlfriend, eh? Dang it, that's just my luck."

Anna caught a firefly and then let it go. She turned to Ruby and asked, "Did y'all talk?"

Ruby replied, "They needed directions here. They both play on Georgie's baseball team this summer, and Brent wanted to know if I ever came out to watch the games. Those two made me weak in the knees. Y'all, we have to go to the next game."

Sandy stood up and looked back to the bonfire—and at Rusty Sanders. Rusty was motioning for her to come back to him. "Nah, I hate baseball fields. They're too dusty, even if the dudes are hot."

Ruby walked over to the cooler and pulled out a drink as Anna and Sandy headed back to the bonfire. As Ruby daydreamed about Reed and Brent, Jerry McDaniel came up behind her and squeezed her bum.

"Ruby Jane, you look sweet enough to eat." Jerry circled his arm around her waist and twirled her around to face him. His eyes were bright and happy while he gently pulled a twig from her hair.

Ruby threw her arms around his neck and went to give him a kiss on the cheek, but he quickly turned, catching the kiss on his lips instead. She giggled. "Hey, Jerry, I thought your family was at Centerhill Lake this weekend." They held hands and walked over to the bonfire.

He grinned mischievously at her, giving her a nudge with his shoulder. "They *are* at the lake this weekend." Jerry inched closer to Ruby, burrowing his face in her hair. "Hey, you wanna come over and watch TV? We could make it by the time *The Tonight Show* starts. So let's get out of here, okay?"

Ruby looked around the bonfire and noticed a few new faces, but most of the people here tonight were her friends from high school. She looked up at him and replied, "Okie dokie, Jerry. But I have to tell the girls. I'm supposed to hang out with them tonight."

Jerry had been one of Ruby's best friends ever since he allowed her to cut in line on pizza day when she was eight and he had just turned nine. He lived a short distance from Everglade Farms and would come over after school to play. Back then, he had been a tall, skinny boy with a buzz cut, and now he was a strapping, six-foot-three hunk. He had shoulder-length blond hair, sea blue eyes, and the cutest dimples on either side of his hopelessly beautiful grin. Half the time they'd been at each other's throats, and the other half, he was trying to stick his tongue down her throat. She loved Jerry; *she just wasn't in love with him.*

Ruby walked over to where Sandy and Anna were standing near the fire. The music and the people were getting louder as the night wore on. "Hey, I just wanted to let you guys know I'm leaving with Jerry, 'kay?"

"Honey, if you don't, I will," Anna said, with a sly smile.

Ruby linked her arm around Jerry's waist as he slung his arm over her shoulder. She looked up at him and said, "Come on, Jerry, let's ride." Jerry pressed his face into her hair and she laughed. "Jerry, stop. That tickles." He lifted his head and threw Anna a peace sign.

As they walked to their cars, Ruby heard Sandy yelling at her in the background. "Don't sleep late. We're going swimming tomorrow!"

RUBY DROVE DOWN ONE OF the curviest roads of Everglade toward Jerry's house. She turned off her radio and rolled down her windows. It was getting late, and most of the people in the homes she passed had already gone to sleep. The steam from the heat of the day rose off the asphalt and caught in her headlights. She heard the crickets and the occasional bullfrog singing in the night air. The full moon was rising higher in the sky as Ruby climbed Campbell Ridge.

As Ruby pulled into Jerry's driveway, she noticed he had flipped on the back floodlights which illuminated the brick ranch-style house, casting long shadows across the yard. Ruby walked along the stone sidewalk and stepped onto the concrete patio that led to the sliding glass doors of the house. She walked over to admire the huge red geraniums and ferns in the clay pots scattered around the perimeter of the patio. There was a black iron patio table and chairs to the far right. The table had a basket of wildflowers as a centerpiece. Ruby inhaled the flowers catching a whiff of lavender and heather. Then she walked through the sliding glass doors without knocking.

Jerry gave her a big hug. "Did you have a hard day at work, honey?"

"Uh huh, I sure did. I'm dying of thirst. Do you have any Cokes or sweet tea?" Ruby plopped down on a barstool, swinging her legs back and forth as she thumbed through the pages of the most recent *People* magazine. Jerry walked over to the fridge and grabbed a couple of Cokes and a big bag of Peanut M&M's. Jerry handed her a Coke and then poured the candy into a big glass bowl and placed it on the coffee table.

Jerry turned on one of the crystal table lamps that flanked the oversized, orange floral couch. Jerry's mom, who spent her First Savings and Loan lunch breaks stealing ideas from the discount furniture store next door, had arranged their den with Sunday afternoon football games in mind.

Jerry grabbed the remote off the coffee table and clicked the television on. He stretched his legs out in front of the couch and motioned for Ruby to sit by him. "Come here, honey bun. Tell me about your day."

Ruby sat down beside Jerry and crossed her legs. She grabbed a handful of M&M's and popped them in her mouth one at a time. "Oh, you know, same ole, same ole. It was busy today. I worked on the display window. I set up the front sale aisle with all the new items for the summer store traffic. And then a couple of shipments came in I had to price and shelf. What did you do?"

"I cut hay in the hundred-acre field. I hope to get the bales up before the rain sets in. I had a few minor tractor issues, but at least the hay is cut."

Jerry flipped to channel four. Johnny Carson had just wrapped up his monologue. Johnny was introducing Angie Dickenson when Jerry draped his arm around Ruby and, scooting her closer to him, began nibbling on her ear. "Mmmm, Ruby, you smell just like pickles."

Ruby laughed so hard her shoulders shook. "I dropped a jar of pickles unloading one of the cartons this afternoon. I thought I cleaned all the juice off. Guess I missed a few spots."

Jerry and Ruby had never been boyfriend and girlfriend in a traditional sense. He had first kissed her at the age of ten. They had been exploring Campbell Ridge and Ruby had reached down to pick up what she assumed was a civil war bullet. She had been turning it over in her hand when, out of the blue, Jerry had kissed her.

Ruby looked up at him, perplexed. "What did you do that for?" She placed her hand on her hips and frowned at him.

Jerry shrugged. "I don't know. You just look sort of cute standing there. Are you mad?"

Ruby shoved the bullet in her bag of goodies and then took a step closer to him and punched him in the arm. "I don't care if you kiss me, but next time, tell me first. Wanna kiss me again?"

Jerry grabbed her bag and placed it on the ground. He looked at her with his lips pressed tightly together. Then shook his head no and turned his back to her. Ruby walked slowly around to face him. He grabbed her quickly and gave her a smooch on the lips. Ruby pushed him back and he fell on the ground. She ran over and jumped on top of him and he started tickling her.

Ruby tried wiggling out of his arms. "Stop, stop, Jerry. You're going to make me pee my pants."

Jerry quickly let her go and rolled away from her and then stood up. He brushed the grass off his pants. "Ruby Jane, don't you know anything? Guys would never kiss girls if you had to ask them first."

From that moment on, Ruby had looked at Jerry differently. Later on in middle school, they had agreed to be kissing buddies, even though neither of them had much experience with kissing. They just made a pact to stay friends no matter what, but would use each other for kissing practice. That had been ten years ago, and they were still practicing.

Tonight, instead of concentrating on kissing practice with Jerry, Ruby's mind kept wandering back to Reed and Brent. Just thinking about those two made her hot as she imagined Reed making love to her on a white sand beach, with the crystal blue water of the ocean crashing on the shore. Then she pictured Brent, with his dangerously sexy eyes, undressing her in a secluded tropical garden with a waterfall cascading over a cliff. The way they had looked at her in the store had set her skin aflame and she had burned all the way to her toes. Ruby had never felt pretty; at best, she was cute on a good day. But Reed and Brent had made her feel pretty—even sexy. Every word out of their mouths dripped with charisma and charm. It didn't hurt that they were both so dad-blame handsome.

Ruby climbed onto Jerry's lap and began to kiss him gently—at first. But she couldn't get Reed and Brent out of her mind. She covered Jerry's mouth with her lips, increasing the pressure, lingering for a deeper taste. Ruby glided her tongue over his teeth. She probed inside his mouth, her tongue circling his tongue. She wanted to drown in the warmth and comfort of his kiss. Ruby was safe with Jerry and knew he would never hurt her. Her hands traveled down his arms, across his muscled chest and around to his back. She wanted Jerry to kiss away the emptiness and longing she felt inside.

Jerry stopped and pulled away from Ruby, looking a bit perplexed. He stared into her half-lidded eyes, so full of desire. "What the heck is the matter with you, Ruby Jane? You've never kissed me this way before. But I'm ready to give you more than kissing if that's what you really want."

Ruby snapped back to reality. She didn't want to hurt Jerry's feelings by telling him the truth—her skin blazed from the flirtatious duo in the store. "I'm sorry. I don't know why I did that. I kinda got carried away."

Jerry squeezed her bottom. "No need to apologize. Just let me know when you want me to give you something more than kissing. I'm ready, been ready for a long time now."

"Hardy, har, har, Steve Martin. I can go home right now if you want me to." Ruby jumped off his lap and grabbed another handful of M&M's.

Ruby noticed Jerry's expression had changed from lighthearted to one of pain. She had told him repeatedly they would never be together sexually. But she had pushed him too far tonight.

He brushed her hair off her shoulder and kissed her forehead. "I'm not trying to push you away, Ruby Jane, but you turn from hot to cold quicker than my shower faucet. Sometimes you act like you really love me, and then other times, I feel like we're brother and sister. It's driving me freaking nuts!"

She *had* hurt him. "Geez, Jerry. I should have realized this thing between us could only go so far. I never want to hurt you, ever, but I can't have sex with you. Sex would ruin our friendship and I won't risk it. I love you, but as a friend, not a lover. You understand? There are so many pretty girls who like you."

Jerry eyes lit up and he tilted his head as he locked her in a death-grip hug. "What pretty girls? Who?"

Ruby didn't exactly know for sure, but she had a hunch. "Anna, for one."

Jerry let go of Ruby and reached for the bowl of candy. "Anna, really? I never even thought she knew I existed." He grabbed a handful of M&M's, tipped his head back and filled his mouth with candy.

Ruby pulled her hair back off her shoulders and then she stretched out across the couch. "Well, for god sakes, don't tell her I said it. Better yet, don't say anything. Just ask her out."

They watched the rest of *The Tonight Show* and then Ruby stood to leave. "Jerry, I've got to go. I'm going swimming tomorrow."

He caught her hand and smiled at her with soft, dreamy eyes. "I'll walk you to your car."

"Okay, Romeo," she said. He walked with her outside to her car holding her hand.

Ruby placed her hand on his cheek and brushed his jawline with the back of her fingers. "Sweetie, I'll talk to you soon, okay?"

Jerry pulled her against his chest, not wanting to let her go. "Aw, Ruby Jane. Sure you can't stay just a little longer?"

Ruby had turned him on in ways she hadn't done before tonight, and she knew better. This was Jerry, for crying out loud. She kissed and hugged him again tightly, then got into her car, and rolled her window down to wish him a goodnight. "Bye, sweet boy."

Jerry smiled as he watched her pull out of the driveway, then turned and walked back inside the house.

On her drive home to Everglade Farms, Ruby's mind drifted back to Reed and Brent again. Out of the two, she had been drawn the most to Reed. He gave her a look like she was moonshine and he was Eliot Ness, which should've been against the law.

When her eyes had locked with Reed's, it had sent a jolt of electricity straight to her stomach, but when Brent had said he wanted to kiss her, and ran his thumb across her hand, white-hot lightning shot down her spine, shaking the ground she stood on.

Why couldn't she be in love with Jerry? They had been friends since they were kids. They were so comfortable with each other. It would have made everything easier. If only she could look at Jerry and feel the raw desire she had when she looked at Brent or Reed, she could be happy for the rest of her life. But, she didn't.

That was it. She realized Jerry was her comfort zone—nothing scary there. Just looking at Reed and Brent scared the daylights out of her.

Chapter 2

Hot Fun In The Summer Time

RUBY'S FAMILY ON HER MOM'S side had owned Everglade Farms since 1802. Growing up on their 200-acre farm, with its rolling hills and wide-open pastures, had been idyllic. The family's two-story, three-bedroom brick house sat on a hill overlooking a pond. Ruby's mother had red, pink, and yellow rose bushes sprinkled throughout their five-acre yard, and her father had planted Japanese elm trees in the early sixties, because they reminded him of his time in the Navy. The fencerow next to their yard was covered with honeysuckle and wild roses.

Ruby had lived here her whole life. Everglade Farms was in her blood. She had learned to ride a bike down the hill of her driveway. She had hundreds of sleepovers with Anna and Sandy. The Glenns and her mom's family, the Campbells, would come to Everglade Farms to celebrate Christmas and Easter. And they would host a huge picnic on Fourth of July with homemade ice cream and fireworks. Ruby would be moving out of Everglade Farms to live with Anna and Sandy in August. Life was changing for Ruby. She could feel it in the air.

Her Grandmother Campbell had passed away before she was born. Ruby had been the only one in the family who had inherited her grandmother's red hair. Her brother, George, was born with dark brown hair and used to tease her growing up, saying she had been adopted. She had her daddy's small, but straight nose with a smattering of freckles, while George had the Campbell button nose.

Ruby had always been a bit of a tomboy, preferring to hang out with her brother, George, and his buddies. George would let her tag along and play backyard baseball or climb up the water tower. The only exception to hanging out with her brother was her best buds, Anna and Sandy.

Ruby languidly stretched out across her four-poster bed, as her mom yelled up the stairs, "Ruby Jane, honey, are you up yet? You *know* Lizzie will be here any minute. Y'all still going swimming, aren't you?"

Ruby yelled downstairs, "Yes, Mother dear, I'm up."

Before Ruby's feet hit the floor, she heard the telephone ringing. Since it was probably Sandy calling, she jumped up and flew down the steps to answer the phone before her mother could reach for it.

"Hello?" Ruby said.

Sandy's voice came through loud and clear on the other side of the line. "It's me."

"Oh, hey, Sandy." Ruby yawned, trying to wake up. She stretched the phone cord from the den to the front door and looked outside for signs of Lizzie.

"Are you up yet?" Sandy asked.

Ruby rolled her eyes. "Yes, I'm talking to you, aren't I?"

"Don't be a smartass. Lizzie will be over any minute."

"Yeah, I know, tell me something I don't know. Hey, Sandy, I gotta go." Ruby fidgeted back and forth, trying to wrap up the phone call.

"I'm heading to your house right now so you don't have to come over and pick me up. I know you're not ready, so get the lead out!" Sandy hung up before Ruby could reply.

RUBY'S MOTHER, LEE, HAD POURED her a glass of OJ and made her cinnamon toast and placed it on the table when Ruby sat down for breakfast. Ruby's granddaddy read his newspaper, while her mama sipped her coffee.

"How was work yesterday? Is Mr. Burns working you to death?" Her granddaddy, Joseph Campbell, loved to tease her.

Ruby drank a little OJ to wash down a bite of toast before replying, "You *know* I love working at the store. Mr. Burns is handing over a couple of the main food vendors for me to negotiate goods for the store." She beamed up at him with pride. "I can't wait!"

He smiled at her with a twinkle in his eyes. "Well, he knows a good thing when he sees it, dumpling." He turned the page and resumed reading the daily paper.

Lee walked over to the kitchen counter to pour another cup of coffee and glanced out the window over the sink. "Sweetie, that'll be a very good experience for you. It'll be one more thing to add to your resume." She walked back to the table and sat down. "Ruby, honey, you can accomplish anything in this life if you are willing to work hard enough for it. I'm so proud of you."

Lee had given up her own career with South Central Bell to raise her children. Ruby didn't think her mother ever regretted it but felt she lived vicariously through her. Her mother had always been Ruby's biggest cheerleader and filled her with confidence.

Ruby rose from the table, cleaned up her dishes, and then kissed them both on the cheeks. Knowing Lizzie should arrive in a few minutes, she ran up to her room to get ready for the pool. Ruby was looking forward to spending some time with Lizzie, whom she loved like a sister. Lizzie and George had gotten married three years ago in a quiet ceremony at the First Baptist Church in Eagleville.

George had noticed the talkative Lizzie his first day of ninth grade algebra and asked her out. They had dated through most of high school. Lizzie had been the lead cheerleader, and George had been the captain of the basketball team. They both had been voted "best looking" in the school annual superlatives.

George, with his darker features, was very different from the blue-eyed, fair-haired, petite and feisty Lizzie. They now lived in Granddaddy's old log cabin next to the main house, which everyone called "The Big House."

Ruby stepped into the shower to quickly shave her legs. She brushed the tangles out of her long hair. She decided to wear her neon pink halter top bikini *because* it showed off her tan, and gave the illusion that she actually had boobs.

Ruby heard Lizzie pulling into the driveway as she threw on her Tom Petty and the Heartbreakers T-shirt, shimmied into her Levi cut-offs, and then grabbed her beach towel and bag. Ruby had just made the last step when Lizzie came inside the back door.

Lizzie said, "Hi y'all! Ruby, are you ready to go, sweet pea?"

Ruby looked at Lizzie's hot, new tiger-print shorts and tube top. The tube top and shorts had tan bands around the legs, waist and chest. "Lizzie, *love* the outfit." Ruby playfully roared like a tiger and struck out with her "claws."

Lizzie blushed, turning several shades of red. "George bought it and a new bikini for me last weekend when we were in Panama City Beach."

Sandy came into the house bellowing, "Hello, Glenn Family! It's another glorious day in Tennessee. Just perfect weather for swimming and catching some rays."

Ruby walked over and gave Sandy a tight hug and then teasingly pushed her friend away. Sandy Cothran and her family had moved to Everglade from Ohio about ten years earlier. They had bought a house a couple of miles from Everglade Farms, and Sandy and Ruby had been fast friends ever since. Sandy had long, shiny chestnut hair that hung to the middle of her back. She stood taller than Ruby at five foot eight, with beautiful wide-set hazel eyes with specks of gold. Going to the pool with Sandy was always a plus. Her vivacious personality and stunning looks always broke the ice for meeting new and interesting people.

Sandy had her beach bag slung over her shoulder and tapped her foot on the linoleum floor. "Come on, guys. Let's get this show on the road. We're wasting valuable sunlight."

The three girls jumped into Lizzie's 1974 black Dodge Charger with a red pinstripe down the entire length of the car. Ruby had called shotgun, so Sandy crawled into the backseat. Ruby wanted to freeze-frame this exact moment in time as they started driving down the road, with their windows rolled down, the radio blasting, and singing at the top of their lungs. Ruby's arm was out of the window, bopping up and down to the music, while the warm summer breeze flowed over her like honey on hot homemade biscuits.

Lizzie broke Ruby's concentration. "How was Ditch Lane after we left?"

Sandy placed one forearm on the side of each front seat and leaned forward. "It was fun. Ruby didn't stay long. She had a date."

Ruby whipped her head around to Sandy. "What date? Are you talking about Jerry?"

Lizzie glanced over to Ruby and then back to the road. "You had a date with Jerry?" Lizzie let up on the gas pedal as they drove through the small town of Eagleville before turning right onto the main highway, which would take them to Henry Horton State Park. The park was situated on the Duck River and offered visitors and locals alike a variety of activities, like swimming, golf, and tennis. The park had a lodge and cabins with a huge playground area where families could picnic and the kids could romp.

Ruby let out a deep sigh. "No, you know better than that. Jerry and I are just friends, although he does come with the added benefit of making out sometimes. I ran into him at Ditch Lane last night and went back to his house to watch *The Tonight Show*."

Sandy nudged Ruby's shoulder, egging her on. "So, who was on Johnny last night?"

Ruby turned around, pulled her shades down over her nose and narrowed her eyes at Sandy. "Angie Dickinson," Ruby said, and stuck her tongue out at Sandy. Ruby didn't share the fact she practically attacked Jerry last night while she daydreamed about Reed and Brent.

Ruby changed the subject abruptly, saying, "Lizzie, I think I'm ready to get on birth control."

Lizzie nearly ran off the road. She looked in her rearview mirror and then pulled onto an old tractor lane. The state road to Henry Horton was always busy. The vast farmlands and Tennessee Walking Horse farms had big horse trailers or tractors coming in and out of the road at all times.

Lizzie placed the car in park and turned to her sister-in-law. With a look of concern, she said, "Honey, I told you I would take you to the doctor when you were ready for the pill. Do you want to have sex with Jerry?"

Ruby crinkled up her nose. "Good god, no! I love him, but I'm not *in* love with him. It's just...I turn twenty in another week. I mean, come on, how many twenty-year-olds do you know who are still virgins? I just want to be prepared."

Sandy pulled out her lip gloss and applied it to her lips. "You're not the only one. Anna is still a virgin."

"Okay, Anna and I are probably the only twenty-year-old virgins left in the county."

Lizzie's hands tightened on the steering wheel, and then she twisted in her seat to face Ruby. "I'll set up an appointment next week with my doctor, unless you would feel more comfortable with your family doctor."

Ruby swore under her breath. "Heck no, I don't want to see my family doctor. He's too good of a friend with Mama. I would feel weird. I think I want my own gynecologist, anyway."

"Okay, I'll call on Monday. Ruby, please take your time to think about your decision carefully." Lizzie turned her head to check for cars before she pulled back onto the highway.

"I have thought about it. It seems here lately that's all I think about. My hormones are out of control. I'll be careful on my choice." Ruby knew having sex was inevitable, and she'd rather be safe than sorry.

A few minutes later, Lizzie pulled into the pool parking lot and circled around twice looking for a parking spot. "I knew we should have left earlier on a Saturday." The pool was packed today.

"Lizzie, don't sweat it. The mommies and kiddies will be heading out for lunch and naps soon and then the pool will be *all* ours." Ruby grabbed up her beach bag and towel with one hand, and with the other one she held onto the door handle because she was ready to hop out.

The girls walked down the sidewalk of the Olympic-sized pool, which sported three diving boards and two slides. They made quite a team, one blonde, one brunette and a redhead. Ruby felt like they were Charlie's Angels, except Charlie didn't have a redhead. Ruby could feel the heat rising and not just from the sun. She could feel eyes on them until they finally made it to their favorite spot, the grassy area in the corner near the deep end of the pool. They laid out their beach blanket and towels and liberally applied Hawaiian Tropic suntan oil.

Oh, how Ruby loved summer! People going off the diving boards, playing Marco Polo, chicken fights in the water, and people laughing—life was truly sweet. Ruby pulled out her battery-operated transistor radio and cranked up WKDF's Rock FM.

Ruby was propped up by her elbows, *lying* out on her back and taking in the scenery when she saw Reed and Brent with one other dude. Ruby stopped breathing. She tried hard to concentrate on what

Lizzie was telling Sandy about decorating the old cabin, but her mind raced. What were the odds Ruby would see Reed and Brent today? Ruby wondered if George or Lizzie had mentioned the pool last night.

Seeing Reed for the first time without a shirt made Ruby unconsciously lick her lips. His muscular chest tapered to his waist in a perfect V-shape, surrounded by bands of muscle. *The Southern sun had tanned his skin to perfection. His swim trunks dipped slightly lower on one side to* reveal just a slice of paler skin. Reed dripped nothing but pure sin as he walked toward them.

Sandy leaned over and whispered in her ear, "Good grief, Ruby Jane, what the heck is the matter with you? If you don't close your mouth you're going to swallow flies."

Sandy made Ruby laugh, because she consistently tried to sound *"Southern" and was always saying something funny.* Ruby glanced at her anxiously. "It's Reed and Brent, Sandy. The guys we talked about last night."

Before she could say anything else, Reed stopped and dropped down, twenty feet in front of her, beside a woman whom Ruby assumed was his girlfriend. The strawberry blonde had a Dorothy Hamill haircut and her boobs were practically falling out of her orange strapless bikini. The girl reached up and linked her arms around Reed's neck, kissing him. Ruby felt a stab of jealousy.

Lizzie said, "You know Reed and Brent both play on George's baseball team."

Ruby turned to Lizzie and said, "I *know*. They came in the store last night. We talked for a few minutes, and they asked me for directions to Ditch Lane because they were looking for George."

Lizzie rolled onto her stomach, laying her face on her hands as she faced Ruby. "Yup, they came out to party with George. You know, you both should really come to one of the games. You'd be surprised how many guys there are on the team this year that y'all could choose from."

Ruby had finally started breathing normally again. "Lizzie, you know I've been busy working all summer, but you can bet your sweet buns I'll be at the next one. When is it?"

"It's Monday night." Lizzie stood up and then motioned for the girls to follow suit. "Y'all, it's scorching hot out *here*. Let's get in the water." Ruby and Sandy both stood up and joined Lizzie as they walked toward the pool. Ruby looked down at the grass, mixed with clover, to search for honeybees. They were harmless unless you stepped on one and then, it stung like the dickens.

Reed glanced up to see the girls and said, "Hey, Lizzie, Lizzie Glenn."

"Why, if it isn't Reed Jackson, as I live and breathe." Lizzie smiled sweetly at him.

Reed threw his head back and laughed, then introduced his friends, Brent, Tammy and Steve. Reed's eyes stayed steady on Ruby as he said, "Hi, Ruby, how are you? Sorry, we missed you at the party last night."

Ruby's stomach flipped and she replied too loudly, "I'm great! I'm sorry I missed y'all."

Ruby glanced over her shoulder to see the summer breeze had blown a strand of Brent's chin-length straight, black hair into his face. He reached up and tucked it behind his ear. Brent gazed into Ruby's eyes. His eyes were framed by long lashes, and he nearly burned her alive with his smoldering look.

Ruby felt her cheeks warm under Brent's intense stare, but she couldn't tear her eyes away from him. She felt this weird magnetic pull between them.

Brent's lips curved into a smile, flashing his pearly whites. "Hey, baby sister," he said in a low, sultry voice.

"Hi, Brent," Ruby said, crossing her arms over her stomach. She slightly bent her knee as she shifted onto her other foot. God, Brent made her so nervous the way he looked at her, with raw desire lingering in his eyes.

Brent absentmindedly rubbed his shoulder. Just then, Ruby remembered overhearing George talk about a player who had suffered a shoulder injury last week. Ruby would bet that player had been Brent.

"Brent, so you're the one who nearly threw his shoulder out last week. How is it?" No doubt her attraction to him was his brooding, good looks. Her stomach flipped again.

Brent swatted at the honeybee swarming at his feet and then lifted his gaze to her again. "Yeah, I'm much better. It still hurts a little. I came to the pool today to work out some of the soreness.

Ruby had the hots for Reed, but Brent's handsome looks and

piercing eyes drew her to him. His olive skin and hairless chest made Ruby want to trail her fingers over what looked velvety-smooth to the touch. There was something slightly mysterious and dangerous about the way Brent smiled at her, and it felt downright exciting.

Brent obviously didn't have a girlfriend—at least not here, anyway.

Ruby said, "Lizzie was just telling us y'all have a game Monday night. Do you think you'll play?"

A confident expression lit Brent's face. "Of course, I'm playing. Are you coming to watch the game?"

As she started to reply she noticed, out of the corner of her eye, Brent's question had sparked some attention from Reed. Ruby got a tingling sensation like something pricking her skin. She thanked God it was hot as blue blazes out here as she felt the blood rushing to her cheeks.

Reed was checking her out again. Ruby shifted uncomfortably. "I'm planning on coming to your game with my friend, Anna. Anna *loves* baseball," she said in a poured-on-thick, sweet Southern belle drawl. Anna had to work today or she would have been at the pool with them. Anna didn't necessarily love baseball, but Anna loved baseball players.

Ruby turned to their friend Steve, who seemed to be dumbstruck by Sandy's beauty. Ruby nearly burst out laughing. She had seen that look from many of Sandy's admirers. It was an "another one bite's the dust" look. "So, Steve, do you play baseball on George's team?"

Steve momentarily glanced over to Ruby and then right back to Sandy, who seemed bored with the whole conversation. Steve replied, "Uh, no. But I do go to the games sometimes."

Reed sat cross-legged on his beach towel and twirled strands of grass between his fingers, then tilted his head up. "I'm glad you're coming to the game, Ruby." Ruby bit her bottom lip as Reed's eyes met hers.

While Reed talked to her, Brent gave him a look that said, "Back off dude." Reed continued, saying, "We need all the cheerleaders we can get."

Tammy elbowed Reed in the chest.

Reed rubbed his hand across his chest and glared back at Tammy like she had lost her mind. "Ow. What was *that* for?" He looked over to Ruby and shrugged.

Brent interrupted Reed, saying, "So, Ruby, do you like going off the diving boards?"

Now this was something Ruby could sink her teeth into. She had been coming to Henry Horton since she was six years old and her father had taught her to dive at ten. "Sometimes."

Sandy drawled in her Yankee-trying-to-be-Southern accent, "Y'all, I'm hawt. Let's get in the water. I don't care if we go off the boards or straight in, as long as it's wet."

Brent stood and Reed looked on. "Ladies, first."

There were two low boards and one high one. As they walked to the boards, Brent grabbed the rails of the low diving board, but Ruby walked past the low board to the high dive and turned to face Brent.

Ruby held the rail to the ladder of the twenty-five-foot diving board and placed her other hand on her hip, challenging him. "Are you game?"

He chuckled, and said, "If you are, I am." His rich laughter warmed her. His silky smooth voice wrapped around her like a warm blanket on a cold night.

The blue water glimmered in the bright sunlight, and the smell of chlorine was very strong. There were only a half dozen or so people in the deep side of the pool. The majority of the swimmers were on the other side of the nine-foot roped area. The high school- and middle school-aged kids ruled the middle of the pool, while the smaller children stayed with their mothers in the baby pool area. Steve and Reed came jogging up behind her and Brent.

Steve punched Brent in his good arm. "We couldn't let you two have all the fun."

Reed walked around Brent, briefly brushing up against Ruby's back to grab the other side of the rail. Ruby felt stings like needles shoot up her spine.

Reed said, "Going off the big one, Ruby?"

Ruby turned and could feel the undercurrent between Reed and Brent, like this was some type of contest. It was odd, she thought, the way those two were acting. Maybe it was wishful thinking, but they both seemed eager to be around her. They had asked her to their ballgames, showed up at the pool and now were practically falling over themselves to stand next to her at the board. She tilted her head and placed her hands on her hips. "It's follow the leader, if y'all are up for it?"

The guys said in unison, "Hell, yes!"

Ruby had always been competitive, and there was no way she would allow these three goobers to get the best of her. She started climbing up the ladder, with the feeling that all three of them were watching her behind.

Ruby got to the top, stood on the board and turned, looking down at them. "It's not too late for y'all to back out."

They laughed, looking at each other like they thought she was nuts.

Brent pushed Reed out of the way, climbing up the board to stand behind her, when the lifeguard blew the whistle and shouted for him to step off the board. He chuckled. "You better show us what you got, Ruby, before we get arrested by the lifeguard police."

Ruby grabbed both sides of the rails, leaned back into her approach, then ran and dove off the high board. Rarely did anyone *dive* off the big board. She had all three elements of a perfect dive: the approach, the flight, and the entry. When her head popped out of the water, she looked up at the mesmerized young men standing near the top of the board and smiled, giving them the thumbs-up. She swam to the side of the pool and pulled herself up and out of the water and then sat on the edge, just in time to see Brent's approach.

Brent stood on the board, tentative at first, but then placed his hands on the bars, leaned back, and then ran and dove off the board. His flight was way off, and his entry into the water hit hard on his very flat, very muscular stomach. Ruby winced for him. One down, two to go. This was getting fun.

Sandy, Lizzie and Tammy came over to the edge of the pool to sit down beside her. They had gone off one of the big slides.

Sandy shoulder-bumped Ruby, and with a quirk of a smile said, "Show off."

Raising one shoulder, Ruby just smiled back at her. "They asked for it."

Brent slowly dragged himself out of the water and sat with them. "Ruby, you creamed us today."

Ruby dropped her eyelids for a split second and then lifted her gaze to meet Brent at eye level. She turned and looked up to watch Steve on the big board.

Steve had a wholesome look about him, with dark auburn hair and a lean body. Just the type of guy any parent would want to see their daughters dating. But right now, he looked like a scared jackrabbit standing up there on the board. She tried very hard not to start laughing. Men were so prideful. Instead of just admitting they couldn't do something, they just went for it. His approach on the board had been atrocious. His flight wasn't bad until his legs flipped over on his entry, and he smacked the water so loudly people turned around to look.

Tammy leaned back and said, "Ouch! Now that had to hurt."

Steve swam slowly over to the side of the pool, but instead of pulling himself up, he decided to stay in the water. "Where in the world did you learn to dive, Ruby?"

With a shrug she replied, "My daddy taught me to swim and dive. I've had a lot of practice."

Reed walked out onto the board, standing there like Ares, the warrior god. Ruby's stomach did a somersault, and then the tingling sensations started at her fingertips and traveled straight down to her toes. Reed's approach was nearly perfect: he stood perfectly straight with no weight on the back of his heels and jumped hard up in the air. His body turned into the dive, with his arms tight to his ears in a streamlined position, his toes pointed and his muscles flexed during his flight. His entry into the water had been completely flawless, and then he swam over to the rest of the gang.

Reed pulled himself up to sit beside Ruby, ignoring the daggers Tammy shot at him. "Ruby, I'm impressed."

Ruby stared at him, dumbstruck. "So am I, Reed."

Sandy stood up. "Come on, y'all, let's swim in an area where we all can have fun—and my feet can actually touch the bottom." Sandy jumped into the deep water and swam to a shallower area.

As Ruby swam underwater, she felt a tug on her ankle and pivoted to see who had her. Reed was pulling her back to him. She pushed off his chest with her foot and swam to the top of the water to catch her breath, with Reed surfacing beside her. She and Reed swam together to the five-foot area. Ruby brushed the hair off her face. Reed darted back under the water, and he grabbed Ruby's ankles, yanking her down under.

Ruby opened her eyes underwater and saw Reed was looking

back at her. His hand ran over her calf and she felt the connection again. But she was quickly running out of breath. She pushed up again with her feet grazing the rough concrete floor and rose until she broke the surface. Reed surfaced right after her, standing so close she could feel his thigh as his muscle tensed. Reed shook the excess water from his hair, spraying water into her face.

She pushed Reed's shoulder and splashed him with water. "What were you trying to do? Drown me?"

Amusement lit his eyes, and Reed replied, "Nah, I was just playing around. You wanna play chicken?"

Brent swam over to them and stood between Reed and Ruby, placing an arm around her shoulder. "Sure, Ruby's on my team."

Brent went underwater, pushing his head between the V of her thighs while his hands gently rubbed along the length of her legs. As he rose out of the water with her on his shoulders, Ruby felt a twinge in her nether regions.

Reed glared at Brent and gave him a chest bump, which nearly knocked Ruby off. "Tammy and I are game." There was definitely something going on between Reed and Brent, as they stared each other down, but Ruby couldn't quite put her finger on it yet.

That left Steve and Sandy, because Lizzie had returned to her beach blanket. Steve smiled at Sandy with a look of pure adoration and said, "I get Sandy!" Ruby almost felt sorry for him. The poor boob didn't have a chance in hell of going out with Sandy because she only dated older guys. And most of those guys were built like Reed and Brent, not Steve. Sandy looked over at Ruby and rolled her eyes. "Oh, good lord. Let's get on with it."

The chicken fights were short-lived because Ruby and Brent won every round, even with Brent's injured shoulder. They had managed to defeat everyone, making them the reigning champions of the day. Brent grabbed Ruby and threw her up in the air, and she came down in a spray of water.

Brent roared with laughter and rustled her hair. "Come on, champ, let's go get something to eat and drink, okay?"

Ruby bent backwards into the water to smooth out her hair. "All right, sounds good to me."

Ruby jogged over to get money out of her beach bag. Reed and Tammy were back lying out on their beach towels. Ruby walked past them, and Reed looked up at her with a scowl on his face. *What was his problem?* She frowned and scowled back at him.

Brent stepped over Reed and Tammy and caught Ruby's hand, linking their fingers together. "You ready to go, sweet girl?"

She glanced down at Reed and Tammy and noticed Reed's expression had turned dark. Ruby said, "Yeah, I'm ready. Anyone else want to come with us?" She needed reinforcements because Brent sort of made her nervous.

Lizzie grabbed her bag. "I do. I need something to eat before I get a headache in this heat." The afternoon had turned almost unbearably hot unless you were in the cool water.

Steve stood up and said, "Me too. I could eat a horse. Sandy, you wanna get something?"

Sandy shook her head no and lay back on the beach blanket, placing her shades over her eyes.

Ruby, Brent, Lizzie and Steve walked to the covered café area to order burgers and Cokes. The radio was playing the top pop twenty-five through the loudspeakers. After picking up their food, they walked over to a vacant table in the shade and sat down. Lizzie talked to Steve while Ruby began to learn more about Brent.

Brent took a big bite out of his burger. He licked the mustard off the corner of his mouth, took a drink and then began moving his straw up and down in his cup. "Do you swim here often?"

Ruby nearly burst out laughing at his line. She wanted to eat but was so thirsty her tongue stuck to the roof of her mouth. She picked up her drink, took a swallow, and then set it back down. "I come at least once a week during the summer."

Brent pointed beyond the pool. "I see tennis courts over there. Do you play?"

Ruby could play almost every sport, but tennis was infuriating. George had tried to teach her, but Ruby had no patience for it. "I play very badly. Is this your first year to play baseball?"

Brent grabbed the napkins as the summer breeze lifted them off the table. A little girl ran over to him and gave him one of the napkins that had flown away. He smiled down at the girl, and she blushed and ran in the opposite direction. Brent used his soda cup to anchor the napkins from flying away. "This is my first year playing on George's team. I used to play baseball in high school, and a couple of times against George. He is one heck of a pitcher."

Ruby took a bite of her burger and then began to nibble on a few French fries. She grabbed for the ketchup at the same time Brent did and their fingers touched briefly. She counted silently to three to let her racing pulse die down. "Yes, George has always been athletic and very competitive. Everyone in my family hates to lose."

Brent belly laughed. "I will attest to that, watching you dive. Dang, girl, you're off the charts!"

Ruby flashed him her pearly whites and playfully nudged his good shoulder. "Well, you're not that great a diver, but you killed it in the chicken fights."

Ruby and Brent were lazily walking back to lie out when Tammy bumped into Ruby, nearly knocking her down and not apologizing. If Ruby had to guess, she'd say Tammy was pissed off about something.

Ruby glanced at Brent and then over her shoulder, watching the diva leave the pool area. "What was that about?"

Brent looked to her lips and, for a brief moment, time seemed to stand still. The sun had peeked out from the clouds, which made the heat blaze. "I believe it was about you, sweet girl."

With an incredulous expression, Ruby asked, "Me? What the heck did I do?"

Brent caught her hand again. They were nearly back to the others, when he said, "Reed has a crush on you."

"I think you must be mistaken. They must have had a fight about something other than me." But the thought of Reed actually having a crush on her had Ruby flipping invisible cartwheels. Something really weird was going on here. Normally, hot guys chased Sandy, and Ruby got the leftovers. But Reed and Brent were both flirting with her, with barely a glance to Sandy—or Lizzie, for that matter. Ruby intended to keep her guard up.

AT THE END OF THE day, Reed watched as the girls drove out of the pool parking lot. Reed hated that he had mentioned to Tammy about his going swimming today. He should have known she would show up. Instead of Reed getting to know Ruby better, Brent had used the opportunity to weasel his way into her graces. Damn it, Brent had had Ruby on his shoulders. Reed had touched those silky legs and wanted them draped around him, not Brent.

Brent and Steve loaded up into Reed's car to head back to Murfreesboro. Steve jumped into the back seat while Brent sat up front.

Brent tossed a glance to Reed. "So, Ruby is hot. This is going to be fun."

Reed turned to Brent before starting his car. "I'm not playing the *Tap It* game anymore. It's been real, and it's been fun, but it's not real fun anymore. Besides, I really like Ruby. I'm going to ask her out, for real."

Brent threw his head back and laughed sarcastically. "Too freaking bad, dude. *I'm* going after her. Besides, you're dating Tammy." Brent shook his head and then ran his fingers through his hair. "Ruby has the sweetest, fullest lips I've ever seen. I was glad we were in the water when she climbed on my shoulders. She had me hooked, brother."

Reed pulled out of the parking lot and onto the highway. As they passed over Duck River, he tossed a menacing glance at Brent and then went back to driving. "I'm not dating *anyone.* Tammy agreed to our set up, no strings attached, period. She got pissed today with me flirting with Ruby. Besides, Ruby is too sweet to fall for you, anyway."

Steve threw his hands back behind his head, leaning back against the car seat with a look of love displayed across his face. "I'm in love with the tall brunette, Sandy. Like, that girl is off the hook!"

Brent lifted an eyebrow. "Dream on, Steve. That chick is way out of your league. I would have gone for Sandy, but when Ruby climbed that big board, it sealed the deal. She is fearless and her ass is hard as a rock."

Reed didn't know why, but it made him extremely mad to hear the way Brent talked about Ruby. "Shut the hell up, Brent." He slowed his car down as they cruised through the little community of Chapel Hill. Cops were always gunning to catch speeders in their fifteen-miles-an-hour speed zone.

Brent glared at Reed as he rolled down the window, placing his arm on the edge. "Dude, you're just jealous. Now, that's something I don't see every day. You just want her for yourself. Well, it ain't gonna happen." He flipped the radio dial until he found a station that would pick up out here in the sticks.

Steve interjected, kindly, "Boys, boys, let's play nice."

Reed didn't say another word on the drive to Murfreesboro. Brent was right—he wanted Ruby. He intended to beat Brent to the punch Monday night if she came to the game.

RUBY EASED BACK GINGERLY TO lie on her bed. Her nose and skin stung from the vinegar bath she had just taken to pull the heat out of her sunburn. She replayed in her mind what had transpired yesterday at the store and today at the pool, with Reed and Brent.

It couldn't be a coincidence that both of them were pursuing her at the same time. Ruby smelled a rat, two very hot rats. Something else, some other factor was at play and she intended to get to the bottom of it. It was time for her to start dealing some of her own cards.

Chapter 3

Knock It Out Of The Park

RUBY LOVED WATCHING GEORGE PLAY sports. He had been an outstanding baseball player in high school, but he had decided not to go to college. Instead, he went to a vocational school where he received an electrical contractor's license, and now he worked with a huge electrical firm in Nashville.

Georgie still loved to play sports. The guys on the baseball team loved George as a coach because he always gave everyone a fair chance to play. Ruby went to several games last year, but tonight would be the first game for her this year. She would have gone much sooner had she known how interesting his roster had gotten.

Ruby telephoned Anna to say she would be picking her up in a few minutes for the ballgame. When Ruby pulled into the driveway, Anna ran out the back door.

Ruby heard Anna yelling to her mother, "Ruby's here, Mama. I'll be home after the game. Love you to pieces."

Ruby and Anna had similar backgrounds. Both of their parents had managed to stay together while so many of their friends' parents were getting divorced. They were both the babies of their families.

Anna Kelly had nearly white blonde hair, which she had cut like Farrah Fawcett's from *Charlie's Angels*. She lit up any room she entered with her infectious laugh and quick wit.

Anna had been Ruby's go-to girl on boy advice since they were sophomores in high school. Ruby trusted Anna's guy-radar implicitly, and tonight's game would require Ruby to call on Anna's exceptional fact-finding skills. Ruby wanted to find out what was going on with Reed and Brent, and if given the chance, Anna would drill it out of them.

Ruby pulled into the parking lot while the teams were completing their warm-up. As Ruby and Anna walked past the visiting team's side, the players whistled at them. Anna smiled at the guys, but Ruby never made eye contact.

Tonight, dust from the field, cigarettes and cigar smoke filled the air, bringing back memories of past trips to George's ballgames. Ruby could smell fresh popcorn and cotton candy. Children ran behind the bleachers playing freeze tag. The warm Tennessee air hung thick with humidity, with an occasional breeze giving only a modicum of relief from the heat.

The first inning was gearing up to start. Ruby could hear chatter of "batter, batter, batter" drifting in from the players in the outfield while the opposing team's first player was getting ready to bat. The towering lights above the field began to pop on as dusk gave way to night.

George's team was on the home side of the field, as Ruby and Anna climbed their way up the bleachers to sit beside Lizzie. Ruby said to her sister-in-law, "Hey, you have great seats!"

Lizzie kissed Ruby's cheek. "I sure do. Y'all *just* made it in time. Anna, I love those sandals."

Lizzie and Anna began talking about the latest and greatest sales at the local Castner Knott department store. Anna slipped off her sandal so Lizzie could try it on. Their conversation became background noise as Ruby scanned the field for Reed.

Ruby finally spotted Reed on third base. She also noticed Brent was playing first base. Brent fielded the ball and fired it to Reed on third as they primed themselves for the start of the game. God, those two guys looked damn good in those uniforms. That alone was worth the drive to the ballpark.

George and the catcher were laughing hard about something, when the umpire came out of the dugout and screamed, "Let's play ball!"

After watching only a couple of innings, this was proving to be one of the most intense games Ruby had ever seen, and she had been watching George play for years. George's team, the Rockies, was in the outfield. The Brentwood Braves had one player already on first base when their shortstop, number thirty-seven, came up to bat and knocked the ball out to center field. The player on first base started running while the ball was still in flight, and he rounded second. As the runner headed toward Reed, the center fielder threw the ball to Reed, who jumped up to catch it and then tagged the runner out.

The third base umpire yelled, "You're OUT!"

The runner started getting into the ump's face, Reed got in the runner's face, and then the gloves were off, and dozens of players from both sides were running onto the field to get into the action or pull their teammates apart.

Ruby dashed to the concession stand for a small bag of ice and paper towels and to check to see if they had a first aid kit. By the time she ran to the dugout, the action was over.

REED WALKED INTO THE DUGOUT to find Ruby holding ice and a first aid kit in her hand. As Ruby's gaze reached him, his stomach did a funny flip. "I'm all right, Ruby." Her cheeks turned pink, which made her more attractive and so adorable. Ruby was very pretty and the fact she didn't get it, by acting insecure around him, made her more appealing.

His bottom lip had been split, and Ruby took ice out of a bag and wrapped it with a paper towel. "Here, now place this on your lip for fifteen minutes so it will help to keep the swelling down and to stop the bleeding." Ruby seemed flustered to Reed as she stumbled over her words. She reached behind her, pulling on her ponytail and twirling it around her finger.

Reed winced when he placed the ice on his lip. "Thanks, Ruby, for the ice."

The way Ruby looked at him, her eyes the color of dark amber with sparks of golden fire, had his breath backing up in his lungs. Standing in the dugout, Reed watched her look straight at his mouth and she seemed to forget what to say next.

George walked into the dugout, threw down his glove, and inspected Reed's lip. "Are you okay, buddy? Well, I don't think you need stitches."

Reed raised his eyebrows, turned his hands up and shrugged. "Nah, I'll be fine. Ruby brought me some ice."

George laughed and looked over to his baby sister. "Hey, little sister, a guy on the other team has a bloody nose and may need a little TLC, too. You think you could help him out?"

Ruby's eyes narrowed and she frowned at George. "Tough titty!" She spun around and walked swiftly out of the dugout.

George snorted, which made Reed cackle and then wince again with pain. "Please stop; you're killing me, George. Thank you, Ruby!"

Reed watched Ruby climb the bleachers to sit by Lizzie and her friend. He could imagine her trim, athletic body, with those long shapely legs wrapped around him, leaving him with a surprising knot of heat in his groin. He'd bet his life she had been aroused before her crazy brother walked into the dugout. His thoughts turned to seducing her, and he couldn't wait until he could ask her out.

Reed's mind drifted back to the pool when he had placed his hand on her calf, her skin so smooth and soft, but so strong. He could feel a connection to her and knew she felt it, too. Then Brent had stuck his damn nose into the equation. It was just a game to Brent. But Reed had felt something toward Ruby he couldn't quite explain or even admit to himself, honestly—he was falling for the brown-eyed honey.

GEORGE'S TEAM WON THE GAME. The players began to gather up their helmets, bats and gloves, then left the field to join families and friends behind the bleachers. Ruby walked with Lizzie and Anna to meet George. He was talking to the Braves' coach, arranging a scrimmage for next Sunday afternoon. George loosely dropped his arm around Lizzie's waist, pulling her close and giving her a peck on the cheek.

The roar of a souped-up Chevy made Ruby and Anna jump. The guy behind the wheel smiled and threw them a peace sign. Anna leaned over to Ruby and said, "I'm going to run to the restroom. You want anything from the concession before it closes?"

"Nah, I want a milkshake. We'll stop somewhere when we leave here." Ruby shoved her hands in her blue jean cutoffs' pockets.

Brent walked up beside Ruby, brushing next to her shoulder. "That was *real* sweet what you did for Reed." He acted mad at her for some reason.

Ruby was alarmed at his tone. "Thank you, Brent. My mama normally does that kind of stuff, but she's not here tonight. That's why I helped out."

Her answer seemed to satisfy Brent, when all of a sudden Reed came up behind her, picked her up, and twirled her around, saying, "Where have you been all my life, Ruby Jane?"

She knew he was joking with her, but it still made her heart squeeze tight. "Reed, put me down, you fool!"

Frowning, Brent crossed his arms so his muscles flexed. "Yeah, Reed, why don't you put her down?"

Ruby got the distinct impression Brent was mad again, but this time at Reed. The look they exchanged between them reinforced her suspicions they were up to something—and it had something to do with her.

Reed slowly and reluctantly put her down, with his hands moving over her. "Thank you, Ruby, my lip is much better. The swelling is down, and the ice stopped the bleeding."

She said politely, "You are very welcome."

Reed began to ask, "Ruby, I was wondering if you would like to go—" Then out of the blue, Tammy came running up behind Reed, placing her arms around his neck and interrupting him.

Ruby thought Reed was on the verge of asking her out before Ms. Priss joined the group. Ruby could only imagine the other girls who were in love with him. She really had to watch her step.

"Reed, I just got here. Were you in a fight?" Tammy reached up and gently touched the corner of Reed's mouth.

Reed pulled Tammy's arms off him and looked back into Ruby's eyes. "Thanks again, and I hope to see you soon, Ruby." Their eyes connected, and electricity charged the air between them. Tammy placed her hand on her hip with a smug look that Ruby wanted to smack off her face. They turned around and walked away.

Brent circled his arm around her shoulder. "So, what are you and Anna getting into tonight?"

Hmmm, oooo-kay, I could dig this too.

Ruby shifted gears since Reed obviously had other plans. "We're going to Sonic for a shake, wanna come?"

All the traces of Brent's anger had simply vanished. "Sure. Would you mind giving me a lift back to my car in Everglade?"

Anna walked up as Ruby replied, "I would be happy to. Where's your car in Everglade?"

Anna looked back and forth between Ruby and Brent, listening as they worked out the details.

Brent shifted his glove from his hip to under his arm. "It's at the high school. You can drop me off at the school after you take Anna home. I just have to tell your brother I'm riding with you."

Hmmm, after she takes Anna home. This sounded more promising by the minute. Brent seemed to be into her, but something felt off, something just didn't feel right. He was drop dead gorgeous, so she should just let it go and enjoy the tingling feeling that radiated through her when she was around him.

Anna looked at her with an "Okay, I know what you're up to" look. "Well, alrighty then, let's go!"

While Ruby drove, Anna fiddled with the radio dials to find a good station and gave Brent the third degree. Does he go to college? Where does he work? Where does he live? Who are his parents? And last, but not least, does he have a girlfriend? The girl had serious skills.

Brent was going into his senior year at MTSU and lived in Murfreesboro. He grew up in Franklin, where his family still lived, and was majoring in engineering because his dad had a small engineering firm in Franklin, where he was supposed to start working after graduation.

Anna had relayed to him their plans for the upcoming semester. But this whole process of Anna's had been to find out if Brent had a girlfriend.

Brent looked over at Ruby and winked. "Are you applying for the position?"

Anna thought he had been talking to her. "Of *course*, I am."

The look he gave Ruby implored "Help me, please."

Ruby nodded at him. "Anna, I do believe our boy Brent here is joking, aren't you, Brent?"

He swiped his hand across the top of his forehead. "Why, yes, I am, Ms. Ruby," he replied in a thick Southern drawl.

At Sonic, they decided to sit at one of the picnic tables instead of eating in Ruby's car. Sonic had music blaring from their speakers, and all of the waitresses tonight wore roller skates. The tables were nearly full when they found one in the back. Ruby and Anna ordered milk shakes while Brent ordered a Coke, cheeseburger, and fries.

Brent sat between the girls and turned to Ruby. "I have some questions of my own since Anna has been giving me the third degree."

Ruby straightened up in her seat and placed her hands over top of each other. "Okay, fire away, Brent."

He cleared his throat. "How old are you?"

Ruby replied with a frown, "Brent Brown, I know your mother raised you better than to ask a lady how old she is. However, since you have been so forthcoming, Anna is twenty and I turn twenty in a few days."

Brent turned to Anna and then back to Ruby. "So, do either of you lovely ladies have boyfriends?" A group of teenage girls sat at the table next to them. They kept looking over at Brent, giggling. He noticed them and gave them a nod of his head. Brent obviously knew he looked good and seemed to enjoy the attention.

Ruby gazed straight into his eyes. "*Non, monsieur, merci beaucoup,*" she said in her best French accent. The waitress brought their orders and Brent paid for it. Ruby took a sip of her shake.

Anna started laughing so hard she choked and coughed. "Good one, Ruby. We went house hunting a couple of weeks ago and found the cutest little place just one street over from campus on Bell Street. For the last two years, Ruby, Sandy and I have been separated in the dorms. We wanted our last two years in undergraduate school to be together. We move to Murfreesboro in mid-August. So where do you and your friends live in Murfreesboro?"

Brent's smile warmed a couple of degrees. "My parents just bought a new duplex off Greenland Drive. I'm moving as soon as the place closes. Steve and Reed have been letting me crash on their couch, so I wouldn't have to sign another lease. They live in the Colony House apartments off Tennessee Boulevard. Brad is another one of our buddies, and he lives in the dorm. He is taking summer classes."

During the banter between Anna and Brent, Ruby remained

silent. She watched him closely, and he kept looking back over at her. There was a silent awareness between them, a burgeoning chemistry developing that made Ruby feel warm inside.

Ruby drove Brent back to his car after dropping Anna off at her house. Ruby had one hand on her steering wheel and her other arm resting on the console of her car. She glanced over to Brent and casually asked, "What gives, Brent?"

His expression turned serious, and he threw her a pickup line that sounded like it had come from a bad movie. "You have grown into quite the beauty, Ruby. I saw you a couple of years ago with George."

With a chuckle, she shook her head. "Does that line really work for you? Or are the girls you normally pick up dingbats?"

His laugh was low and masculine. "What do you mean?"

Ruby came to a four-way stop. She looked both ways before she took a left back onto Old Everglade Road. "I'm not a rocket scientist, but when two hot guys are fishing in the same lake, trying to reel in the same fish, they may need to switch bait 'cause this fish ain't biting."

Brent cracked up at her comment. "You're one smart cookie."

She replied wittingly, "My daddy didn't raise no fool. So 'fess up, spill the beans."

Ruby remained silent while Brent relayed the rules of *Tap It*. When they arrived at the high school, Ruby parked beside the only car left in the parking lot, a silver Camaro. "So you mean to tell me y'all have been playing this game for the last three years, and no one has caught on? How many girls?"

Brent looked at her sheepishly. "Yeah and, uh, well, not that many girls really, maybe four or five."

"Pretty shallow stuff. Well, thanks for telling me. I'll check ya later," Ruby said, dismissing him.

Brent leaned over to her, cupped her face so gently with his hands and turned her to him. Something about him felt threatening to her, and she could barely breathe. Brent's cheeks had darkened. "Ruby, I like you, a lot. I want to go out with you. I told you the truth. Go with me to dinner and a movie this weekend?"

She held her breath, debating whether she should go out with him. "Brent, I'll play your little game, but as a player not a pawn. I'll go out with you, Saturday night. Be at my house at seven. This is going to be fun." Ruby had just changed the rules of the game.

Brent tensed, and then replied, "All right, I'll pick you up at seven. May I kiss you, Ruby?"

She shook her head. "No, Brent. It's not going to be that easy. You're going to have to work for it. This has definitely been an enlightening night. I have to work tomorrow, so I'll see you this weekend. Do you know where I live?"

He pressed his lips against the back of Ruby's hand. "I do. I'll see you Saturday night."

Ruby had been right. Reed and Brent had had the intention of playing her for their own amusement. She felt obligated to play the *Tap It* game, for all of the girls who had been clueless. Brent's next move was coming Saturday night. She couldn't wait to see how Reed would play the game. Ruby heard her mother's voice in her head: "Be careful playing with fire, honey. You may get burned."

THE NEXT EVENING RUBY LOCKED the door to the general store, placed the key in her purse and turned to walk down the steps. Mr. Burns had left early to take his wife out to dinner in Murfreesboro. The parking lot was lit by a lone security light and the moon. The wooden structure of the store was sheltered by two massive pin oak trees that cast shadows across the lot. The grass around the store had been freshly mowed. The night air still felt hot and muggy. The lightning bugs had come out to greet the night.

Ruby looked across the parking lot and saw Reed leaning against his car door with his arms crossed. Ruby's stomach flipped upside down at seeing such an arousing display of his biceps. This must be Reed's next move in the game. She should have been sharpening her mental skills, but her brain had just turned to mush. It was hard to think rationally when she was around Reed. On the flip side, Ruby had decided to enjoy the attention from Reed and Brent, with their little dating game, because she didn't know how long it would last.

"What are you doing here?" Ruby asked nonchalantly. Her legs shook and her insides throbbed.

Reed uncrossed his arms and walked over to greet her. "I thought I'd just stop by and see what was going on tonight."

"Reed, do you like me? I mean, really like me?" Ruby blurted out. The surprised look on Reed's face gave her the impression she had caught him off guard. *First blood, baby.*

"Yes," Reed replied with caution. "I'm very attracted to you."

Ruby frowned at him and swatted at a mosquito on her arm. "Reed, the jig is up. I know all about *Tap It.*" Ruby stopped walking and turned to him. She kept her eyes on him and couldn't wait to hear his reply.

He flinched when she mentioned the game. "Just what did Brent tell you about *Tap It?*"

She tried to sound smug and raised one shoulder. "Brent told me everything."

His eyes flamed, making them the color of whiskey. He took another step closer to her and she could feel the warmth of his breath. "Did he tell you I didn't want to play the game or did Brent conveniently leave that out?"

Touché—she had not expected that Reed didn't want to play the game. Maybe he really did like her. Or maybe this was a different angle to his move. Either way, she wasn't letting her guard down for one minute. A car passed by the store, and when the driver honked the horn, she waved.

With a look of unconcern, Ruby adjusted the strap of her purse, which had slipped off her shoulder. "Don't sweat it, Reed. If you and Brent want to play, I'm game. *Tap It* sounds fun. Besides, you're gorgeous. And it's not like I'm looking for a boyfriend, anyway."

Reed's eyes still flamed, but he replied, coolly, "Good to know."

Ruby noticed his shoulders tense. He made another step closer, leaning down to her face. She could feel the heat coming off him and, god, he smelled *male*. Reed was going to kiss her. She closed her eyes, parted her lips, and waited.

Ruby opened her eyes and instead of kissing her, he took a step back. With a lifted brow, he said, "I didn't ask you out."

Ruby's eyes flashed wide open and her cheeks fired blood red. She had been played. Her eyelids dropped for a second and then narrowed her eyes at him. She stepped in closer, so close she could see the pulse race in his throat. She squared her shoulders, bracing herself after the barb of his words. Her fingers tingled as she balled her hands into fists. "Fine, then you won't be wasting my time or yours." She turned abruptly and walked to her car.

Reed swooped in, dropping his arm around her waist and pulling her next to the length of him. Ruby's back pressed against the rock wall of his chest as he buried his face in her hair. His scent made her female muscles quiver deep inside her low belly. A hint of his aftershave mixed with his sun-warmed skin and a trace of sweat had sent her pheromone detectors into maximum overdrive. He drew in a sharp intake of breath and a deep throaty moan escaped his lips.

He murmured, "Don't."

Reed kissed her neck in the place right below her earlobe and chills ran up her spine. Ruby relaxed as her head fell back and tilted against him. She wasn't the only one aroused, she thought, feeling the press of his buckle next to her bum—and so much for keeping her guard up. Ruby told herself she should be running for the hills. Her mind screamed this was just a part of the game. But her body had turned traitor, her legs grew weak, and her breaths became short and shallow.

REED TRACED HIS FINGERS ALONG her side, barely grazing her breast. Her pert nubs stood to attention. Blood was pounding in his veins as Reed turned her around to face him. He had intended to teach her a lesson about the damn game, but now he was the one being schooled. He found himself lost in her eyes.

"I thought you didn't want to ask me out." Ruby placed her hands at his waist and looked into his eyes, waiting for an answer.

"I don't want to ask you out," he teased, pressing her against him.

"Okay, so what do you want?" She lifted a brow as her fingers ran up the muscled ridges of his back. Reed felt the hammering of her chest next to his. The heat between them was increasing and knots jerked tightly in his groin.

Reed leaned forward, pressed his lips on her forehead and said, "This."

She tensed when he kissed her, and then he kissed her again, this time on the tip of her nose. "This." The desire coiled tightly in his low belly every time his lips touched her.

He whispered, "This," as he kissed her lips, lightly, gently. He shifted slightly, kissing the corner of her mouth, and her lips parted again. Reed had won the first battle when she gave in to his light, feathery kisses.

"Do you like that, princess? Do you want to kiss me?" His mouth was just barely touching her lips.

Ruby's amber-gold eyes glowed wild with desire. She answered raggedly, "Please, Reed."

Reed dropped his head forward. His mouth slanted over hers and devoured her with his kiss. Ruby smelled of lust and sexual hunger. She also smelled of rebellion, yet she seemed so full of angst.

RUBY BROKE FROM HIS KISS and ran her fingers gingerly along his chiseled jawline. She ran her fingers down the column of his neck and stopped against the rippling muscles of his chest. She tilted her head and began kissing and sucking his neck, trailing her tongue along his salty, spicy skin. His thigh tensed against hers.

Two can play this game, she thought. She deeply breathed in the smell of him as she grabbed his butt, pressing him next to her. Ruby's lips ran softly back and forth against his neck, and then she ran her tongue up to his earlobe. The man had insane charisma, drawing her to him like a moth to a flame, and she murmured, "Do you want to kiss me?"

Reed tilted her chin up and said, "Hell, yes, I want to kiss you." His delectable mouth was half open, breathing fast, and his dark eyes flared dangerously.

Ruby stared up at him with half-lidded eyes, so full of desire. She was breathing as fast as he was. Reed covered her mouth with his, exploring her lips, moving his tongue in and out of her mouth like a finely tuned musical instrument and she was the notes to his song.

He kissed her slowly and deeply at first, and as the kiss grew longer, she felt his pulse speed up. She felt the quickening in his chest as she quivered underneath his touch. Ruby was spinning out of control. Her senses sizzled and crackled like sparks on the Fourth of July.

Reed grabbed her hair, twisting it in his fingers. "You're so sweet, honey. Sweeter than anything I've ever tasted before."

His words had nearly made her convulse on the spot. She shifted her legs as heat rushed between them. She felt nothing but pure pleasure roll off her in waves.

She released a throaty sigh and wet her lips. "You are driving me crazy."

Reed trailed kisses over her ear and replied in a rich, Southern drawl, "God, woman, you're the one driving me nuts."

Ruby leaned back against the car, trying to catch her breath. "Wow, Reed, you're a really great kisser."

He chuckled, brushing her hair back, off her shoulder. "Not too shabby, yourself. You wanna grab a pizza and movie Saturday night?"

"Can't, Saturday night." Maybe she needed to call Brent and cancel her plans with him, but she quickly thought this could be a part of the game.

He grimaced and his eyes became stormy. "Why not, do you have to work?"

"No." This conversation was definitely going to ruin her very delightful mood.

He stared at her, his expression darkening. "You're going out with friends?"

"Sort of," she answered, reluctantly. Ruby shifted her feet; she felt guilty all of a sudden.

His face clouded with disappointment and his voice became rough. "Well, let's not play cat and mouse, honey. Spill it."

Ruby pushed her hands in her blue jean pockets and looked up at him. "I have a date."

"With?" His eyes were boring a hole through her.

She furrowed her brow. He wasn't making this easy on her. "Are you going to make me say it?"

He clenched his fists. "Hell, yes, with whom?"

"Brent." This was their game, not hers, dad blame it.

Reed shook his head and turned, walked three steps away from her, then stormed back to stand in front of her. His breaths were hard and uneven. "You're still determined to play this damn game, aren't you?"

"Aren't you?" She had fire in her eyes. Reed and Brent had picked her out in the store. They had decided to make her a part of the game. This hadn't started with her—but she was going to finish it.

His fingers trembled, and his lips thinned into a sneer. "No, I'm not, but if you're so fired up about it, go on with your date with Brent. See if I give a shit."

He turned away, and she reached out to stop him by placing her hand on his forearm. "We could get pizza Friday night?"

His muscles flexed and he removed her hand. "I don't think so, Ruby. Call me when you're through with Brent." Reed walked over to his car and opened the door.

"Wait! Is this another part of *Tap It*? Kiss me senseless and turn me away. *Very* clever."

Reed placed his hand on top of his car. "This isn't a game to me, damn it."

Ruby stood with her hands on her hips. "Yeah, that's what you said. Why should I believe you?"

He combed his fingers through the silky strands of his hair. "You don't have to believe me. That's your choice. Bye, Ruby."

Their eyes connected and held for a long second, and then he was gone. Reed either really cared for her or this was a very calculated move in *Tap It*. He had been playing the game for three years. If she had told him she wouldn't date Brent, then the game would have been over, before it even began. She would lose. If he was telling her the truth, then she already had.

Chapter 4

Stuck In The Middle With You

RUBY LOOKED FOR BRENT TO arrive any minute. Tonight made her nervous. All week at work her mind drifted to the encounter with Brent at Everglade high school and with Reed in the store parking lot. They both made her hot and restless. She had felt such desire in Reed's kiss, and he made her feel like a woman. The memory of his kiss burned inside her. Tonight, she needed to shake her thoughts of Reed, because she was going out with Brent.

Ruby wore a new pair of Turtle Bax blue jeans and a lilac halter top. She curled her hair for a change—nothing too dramatic, just enough to give it a little bounce. Ruby hated wearing makeup but placed a little amber shadow on her lids to compliment her perfectly arched eyebrows and swiped dark brown mascara across her lashes, which set off her doe eyes. She looked in the mirror and decided this was the best she could do with the goods God gave her. She applied a little pink lip gloss, dabbed a drop of Halston behind both ears, and slid on her flip-flops. She walked outside to sit on the porch with her granddaddy, to wait for Brent.

For as long as Ruby had been alive, on Saturday nights her granddaddy, when the weather permitted, sat outside on the front porch and listened to the WSM radio broadcast of the *Grand Ole Opry*. She sat down beside him on the porch swing, and the family dog, Max, came running up the steps to meet her. Max was a Doberman. He had always been the most loving dog, even though he looked like a killer.

Her granddaddy looked over at her. "You have such a pretty face, Ruby Jane, so why are you always trying to cover it up?" He liked her to wear her hair tucked behind her ears; she didn't.

She gave him a big hug. "Granddaddy, I love you. You always make me feel pretty. I just wish I could believe it myself."

The summer breeze on the porch felt warm, but thankfully the humidity was low. Summer in Tennessee could be exhaustingly hot and humid, but this evening felt very nice.

A few minutes later, Brent pulled his Camaro into the driveway and drove up the hill. Ruby's nerves were making her body shake like a leaf on a tree. She kissed her granddaddy and stood up.

He stretched out his cane to rub Max behind his ears. "Is this a new beau coming up the drive?"

Ruby gave him a meaningful glance. "Yes, sir. I'll just walk out and meet him. We'll be back soon."

She and Max walked along the sidewalk and down the steps toward the back of the house where Brent had parked his car.

Brent stepped out of his car and looked straight at Max, and then he froze. "I see you brought your guard dog." Max trotted around Brent, smelling him, and then peed on his car tires.

Ruby choked back a laugh. She knelt down to her dog and scratched his ears, while he tried to lick her face. She backed away from Max, so she wouldn't have to reapply her make-up. "Max? He's a sweetheart. Come here and let him smell your hand."

Brent looked afraid, backing up to his car and placing his hand on the door handle. "Are you crazy? What if he decides to take a bite out of it?"

Ruby said with a perfectly straight face, "I promise he won't. Trust me?"

He hesitated. "I guess I'll have to." Brent slowly approached the dog and allowed Max to sniff his hand. Max promptly licked him and then began wagging his little stub of a tail.

Ruby smirked. "See, a big ole pussy cat."

Brent relaxed and let out a raspy sigh. "Hello, sweet girl, you look very beautiful tonight." He pulled her up into his arms.

Max let out a low growl, and Brent quickly let her go, throwing his hands in the air. "Good doggy."

Ruby cackled and bumped her shoulder against his. "Well, you know dogs are really good at sensing danger."

"Ha, ha, ha, Ruby," he said, and then carefully put her hand in his and glanced down at Max, who was back to wagging his tail.

With a sideways glance, she added, "Oh, and by the way, you look beautiful, too."

Brent shook his head, and his mouth twitched in amusement. "Ruby, you crack me up. Do you always say what's on your mind?"

Ruby shrugged. Brent was incredibly good-looking any night of the week. She didn't have to lie about it. "Mostly... Did you have any trouble finding us?" It would be hard to get lost in Everglade.

"Not really. I've been at the school so I sort of had an idea where I needed to turn. I almost missed it when I remembered to take a right beside the gas station onto Concord Road." Brent took a deep breath. "*God,* Ruby Jane, you smell good."

She caught him glancing down her halter top. Having him near her made it difficult to think. The wind rustled the leaves in the trees, and Max shot off in the yard after catching scent of a rabbit running along the back of their house. "Come on, I want you to meet someone."

Brent wrinkled his nose and cocked his head to the side. With a look of distaste he asked, "Who, your father?"

Mischief danced in her eyes. "Not yet, he is at a Ruritan meeting tonight. Dad's group does a lot of work for the community. He won't be home until late. I want you to meet my grandfather. He is eighty-six years old, and he is the love of my life."

Brent stopped her for a moment, and his eyes made her stomach muscles clench. His expression softened. "I would love to meet him. The movie doesn't start until nine o'clock."

Ruby felt more aware of Brent than she wanted to reveal. The physical attraction she felt toward him was strong, from his incredible eyes to the solid muscles of his chest. They held hands while they walked back to the front of the house.

Ruby introduced her granddaddy to Brent, and he began to tell Brent of her childhood antics. The stories made Brent belly laugh on several occasions. She watched silently and realized the two of them were comfortable with each other, and it made her happy.

Her granddaddy stood and said, "Well, I'll leave you two

lovebirds alone. I'm sure your mama will need some help cleaning up the supper dishes. It's been nice to meet you, Brent." He turned around to go, but then stopped, looking back at her date. "Brent, this girl is very special to this family. If I were you, I would remember that." Her grandfather turned and walked inside the house.

Ruby was dying now, a slow, painful and embarrassing death.

BRENT BARELY KNEW RUBY, BUT he wanted to know all about her, even if it meant cultivating a relationship with all of her family members. "I suppose I better watch my step around you."

Brent playfully cringed in fear, and she gingerly smacked the side of his arm. She planted her hands on her hips. "Yes, you better, because my daddy is much worse."

Brent wrapped his arm around Ruby, moving her a little closer to him on the porch swing. They began to slowly rock in the swing in silence. Brent closed his eyes, inhaling the lavender and roses in the landscape, which, mixed with Ruby's perfume, was a heady combination. They listened to the radio, still tuned to WSM. The *Grand Ole Opry* hour had ended, and tunes from Emmy Lou Harris wafted through the warm summer air.

Brent's need to touch her had his blood running hot. Ruby's perfect oval face and her creamy peach skin were begging to be touched by him. He wanted to feel her soft, full lips under his. He wanted to feel her trim, athletic body molded against his. Brent could imagine her quick, short breaths, and he became feverish with want for her. He bent over and placed his mouth gently on her lips.

Brent could feel Ruby trying to pull away from his kiss, when he flicked his tongue inside her warm mouth, which lit him up in a sea of flames. Then Ruby embraced him, returning his kiss with the same passionate heat and sending a tremor through him.

Ruby was taut as a bow, as she dragged in a ragged breath and looked into his eyes. Brent could see she hungered for him, as much as he did for her. He buried his face in the soft skin of her neck, and each time he came back to her mouth, his desire increased with reckless abandon. Ruby ran her fingers through his hair, nuzzling her cheek against his face. Brent wanted to rip her clothes off and make love to her right there on her front porch swing.

He held her against his chest, and could feel the tight beads of her nipples through the thin fabric of her halter top. "Sweet girl, I want you so bad." Brent could feel Ruby's heart pound against him, and the force of it made him tremble. Hellfire and damnation, they were on her front porch, and her mother and grandfather were inside!

Suddenly, the porch light flipped on, and Brent felt like he had been scalded with hot water. Ruby jumped as though she had been doused with cold water, and Max jumped up from sleeping and began to bark.

Ruby laughed in nervous surprise. "That scared me to death. I felt like I was sixteen, not twenty. Are you ready to head into town?"

"Best idea I've heard all night." Brent shifted uncomfortably in his blue jeans.

ON THE DRIVE INTO TOWN, Ruby thought about Brent's kiss. She didn't feel the passion she had felt with Reed when he held her in his arms. But she did feel passion and could feel Brent wanted her. They had been in a pretty heated make-out session when her mom flipped on the front porch light. She wondered how long her mother had been watching them, before she had finally turned on the light. Ruby's face flushed at the thought of it.

By the time they parked and walked up to the theater, a line had formed. While Ruby and Brent stood in line at the theater to buy tickets, she glanced over to the concession stand and froze. A spike of ice landed like a thud in the middle of her chest. Reed and Tammy were buying popcorn and Cokes. She flushed with heat. Ruby had made the right decision. Reed was still seeing Tammy.

Brent stepped up to the theater counter and paid for their two tickets. He turned to Ruby and noticed her looking inside the door and followed her gaze. "Hey, you wanna see what movie they're seeing? Maybe we could all sit together."

She flinched slightly. Great, that's all she needed—to sit with Reed and his prissy, perfect princess. She lied through her teeth. "Sure, whatever you want to do is okay with me."

They walked up to Reed and Tammy. Reed met Ruby's gaze and held it for a second too long. Out of the corner of her eye, she had seen Brent's reaction and noticed the muscle in his jaw ticked.

"Hey, y'all, I didn't realize you were coming to the movies tonight. We could've double dated." Brent put his arm loosely around Ruby's shoulder.

Reed shot him a look that could kill, but then his expression relaxed. "Tammy and I are seeing *Star Wars*. What about you two?"

Ruby linked her arm around Brent's waist. "That's what we're seeing, too. Y'all want to sit with us?" She fixed her eyes on Reed, not looking away once. Damn him, and he had given her grief about Brent.

Reed only glanced at Ruby and then ignored her completely. He turned to Brent. "Hey, man, if it's cool with you, then it's cool with us." Reed placed a kiss on the top of Tammy's head and then tilted her chin up to his face. "Is that okay with you, honey?" He emphasized the word "honey."

Tammy, clueless to what was going on between the three of them, said, "Sounds like fun to me. Ruby, you want to go to the restroom before the show starts?"

Oh, joy! Ruby glanced over to Tammy, and then she reached up and kissed Brent. "Would you mind getting me a Coke and some peanut M&M's? I'll be right back, *honey*." In her peripheral vision, she saw Reed frowning. A wicked smile curved Ruby's lips and she walked off with Tammy.

Tammy hooked her hand on Ruby's elbow. "So, you're going out with Brent? He is so gorgeous."

"It appears that I am." Ruby followed her inside the restroom. The last thing she wanted to hear was anything about Tammy and Reed's relationship.

Tammy applied lipstick and then brushed her hair, looking at Ruby in the mirror. "We're both lucky to have such gorgeous hunks by our side. If Brent is anything like Reed, you'll be sore in the morning." Tammy gave her an evil grin. Then she offered Ruby her lipstick. "It's Reed's favorite flavor."

Was Tammy deliberately trying to provoke her? Make her sore, indeed, the little hussy. Ruby shook with anger but concealed it. Ruby took the lipstick and applied it to her lips and then grabbed a towel to wipe it off. "Yuck! It may be Reed's favorite, but it isn't mine. What flavor is this anyway, licorice? I prefer cherry." Ruby pulled her cherry lip gloss out and applied it to her lips. "See, much better, but then again, you have to have lips to wear this color. Here, wanna try some?" Ruby saw sparks of fire shoot from Tammy's eyes.

As they made their exit out of the restroom, Ruby locked arms with Tammy. "I believe we're going to be great friends. Don't you?" Ruby preferred the "kill 'em with kindness" approach.

Ruby and Tammy joined the guys at the entrance to the theater. Ruby's hands were trembling when she looked between Reed and Brent. The silence that hung between the four of them was as thick as the ice in a hockey game, and she had the winning goal. Reed and Tammy walked into the theater.

Brent handed the Coke and candy to Ruby. "After you, sweet girl."

Midway down the aisle, Reed motioned for Tammy to enter a row. Then Brent pointed for Ruby to follow Reed. *Dad blame it!* Ruby had to sit between Brent and Reed for an entire feature-length film. Static electricity bounced off Reed and Brent. It made her silently chuckle. The Force wasn't with her, but she was sitting between it. She was so nervous, she woofed down her M&M's before the movie trailers finished.

Brent leaned over and asked, "You want some more candy?"

"No, I think I've had enough chocolate for today." She took a sip of Coke and placed the cup on the floor, at the same time Reed bent down. Their arms touched and she sizzled from the heat of it.

Reed had accidentally knocked her soda over. He stood and said, "I'll go get you another one."

Brent interrupted, "No, I will. Be back in a jiffy." He jogged back up the aisle.

Ruby took in a deep breath and sighed. Reed leaned back in his seat and crossed his arms. Ruby squirmed in her seat, replaying Reed's kiss. She tried to focus her mind on the big screen and didn't dare turn to look at him, for it would have betrayed her thoughts.

Ruby felt Reed's fingers trail down her arm. He began to make small circles on her side, nearly brushing against her breast, and she stiffened as tingles shot up her spine. Reed was playing her in the theater. She could play that game and teach him a lesson. She crossed her arms and gently traced her fingers against the back of Reed's, and then she grabbed his fingers and twisted them so hard he jerked away, elbowing Tammy in her arm.

"I'm so sorry, Tammy. Are you okay?" he whispered, but started chuckling.

Tammy leaned over and replied, "What is wrong with you?" Behind them they heard, "Shh!"

"Nothing's wrong. I had a muscle spasm." Reed turned behind him and scowled and then glanced at Ruby, but she stared straight ahead at the screen while a slow grin played across her lips.

AFTER THE MOVIE, THEY ALL walked outside of the theater and Reed asked Brent, "Y'all want to go get a pizza and have a couple of beers?" The theater parking lot was still full of people who had filed out of the theater doors. The traffic on Broad Street was humming with cars, and in the distance, a train whistled as it rolled along the tracks.

As they approached the car, Brent cupped her chin with his hand, tipped her face up and planted a crushing kiss on her. Then he drew back and smiled at her. "It's up to you, sweetheart." He stroked her hair with his hand, resting it on the small of her back.

Ruby blinked a few times before smiling back at Brent. She had been momentarily stunned by his dreamy kiss. She almost forgot that Reed and Tammy were watching them. She was giddy with excitement. "Sure, why not?" Ruby fought hard to appear normal, but there was nothing normal about Reed and Brent. They both knew the score, and she was stuck in the middle.

They went to Sir Pizza and sat in the corner booth in the back of the restaurant. Brent ordered a pitcher of beer. Ruby whispered in his ear, "I don't like beer. Would you order me a Pepsi?"

Brent placed his hand on top of hers and rubbed gently. "Sure. One Pepsi, too," he added to the order.

Reed poured himself a mug of beer and drank it rather quickly. Tammy chuckled. "Thirsty, Reed?" Tammy laughed and poured herself a mug of beer.

Reed held Ruby's gaze for a long second, before she turned away. This time before Brent could see the longing in her eyes. Reed knew she liked him and he was obviously trying to make her jealous with Tammy.

How did Brent and Reed do it? For three years, they had used women in this game, and she could barely get through one night. She had not been playing *Tap It* for a week yet. She still didn't know all the rules to the game, but she had to get both Brent and Reed to profess undying love for her to win, and the game was beginning to get on her last nerve.

If Reed had never stopped by the store and kissed her, she would have had a wonderful date with Brent tonight. But Reed had, and sitting across from him made this whole scene terribly uncomfortable for her. She couldn't lie to herself, she was jealous of Tammy. Reed had rocked her world.

Tammy prattled on about mundane topics: her hair stylist, her nails, how her daddy refused to give her more money until next week. Tammy was applying lipstick at the table, for crying out loud—with her makeup mirror, no less. She made Ruby want to puke.

Ruby fumbled her hand in the side zipper of her purse until her fingers caressed the piece of amber. She carried it with her everywhere. The stone had a calming effect on her. She couldn't explain how it worked, but the amber stone gave her strength. She began to breathe easier, released the stone and zipped it securely back in her bag.

Brent finished his beer and placed his hand on Ruby's thigh, gently rubbing back and forth. "Did you like the movie?"

Ruby glanced over at Reed to see his jaw clenched shut. Reed looked at her like he knew what she looked like naked and it scorched through her dad-blame clothing, straight to her bones. Ruby had to admit, at least to herself, Reed and Brent's attention secretly thrilled her. She tipped her head back to Brent and bit her bottom lip. "Yeah, it was good. I really liked Han Solo."

"Oh, you did, did you? Han Solo is pretty cool." Brent chuckled and poured another beer as the waitress placed their pizza on the table.

Ruby rested her hands on top of the table. "And he is not bad to look at, either." She grabbed a slice and took a bite, closing her eyes. "Mmmm, this is so good. I didn't realize I was so hungry." Then she grabbed another slice for her plate.

Reed and Brent both looked at her funny, both of them seemingly enjoyed watching her woof down her pizza. Ruby guessed their normal dates didn't eat like a field hand, but she was starving. "What can I say, I love to eat!" They both laughed at her, while Tammy picked at her slice.

After Ruby's third slice, she rubbed her tummy and leaned back against the table. "Now, I'm ready to go to sleep."

Reed and Brent were talking about their next baseball game. The Rockies had a real chance of winning the season. Ruby glanced at Tammy.

Tammy had finally taken a real bite of pizza and drank a sip of beer. "This is very good, isn't it? I don't eat pizza too often. It's so fattening."

It took Ruby a second before she realized she had been hit. *Why, that little heifer!* Ruby guessed Tammy wasn't as dumb as she looked. Since Ruby worked all her fat off, she decided to be a glutton and grabbed one more piece. "I wouldn't know. I can eat all day and not gain a pound. Guess it's just good genes."

Brent and Reed picked up on Ruby's sarcasm and started laughing. Brent squeezed her knee, and as his hand traveled to the V of her jeans, she clamped down on his hand. He leaned toward her and inhaled the smell of her hair and then grabbed his mug and raised it to Reed. "To Ruby's hot damn jeans!" He turned to Ruby and winked.

Reed picked up his mug. "To Ruby's hot damn jeans!" Then he winked at her with a slow and sexy grin, curving his delicious lips. Geez, they had this game thing choreographed.

Ruby felt satisfyingly smug when she glanced over at Tammy, who looked madder than a rattlesnake.

Chapter 5

Rock The Boat

REED HAD NOT PURSUED HER again after that night at the movies. Ruby would not allow her feelings for Reed to make her miserable. Instead, she made the decision to move on with her life. Brent wanted to spend time with her, and she genuinely enjoyed his company.

Brent invited her to spend the Fourth of July at his grandfather's cabin on the lake. The cabin was nestled atop a cliff overlooking the lake, surrounded by dense woods. They pulled into the driveway, parked and began to unload their baggage and groceries.

The kitchen counter was stuffed with food after they had brought in the groceries and laid out the nonperishables, and Ruby wondered how in the world they would eat it all.

Brent opened the sliding glass door and walked onto a huge deck overlooking the lake. "Man, you have to come out here and see this sunset."

Ruby placed the last of the groceries in the pantry and joined him on the deck. She watched the fiery sun descend behind the mountains. There were only a few clouds scattered across the sky. The sun melted to orange, red and pink, until nothing was left but darkness. Then, one by one, the stars came out to wink at Mother Earth.

Below the cliffs, several boats were cruising down the channel with their lights on. Ruby inhaled the fresh night air and rested her head against Brent's shoulder. She said, "It's so serene, so majestic."

Brent kissed her sweetly on her lips and held her tightly in his arms.

Brent gave her the master bedroom with a sliding glass door which led to the wraparound porch. He sprawled across the bed as Ruby placed her clothes in the drawers. He wore a pair of blue-jean cutoffs and a Rolling Stones T-shirt. Brent was seriously cute and looked like a teenager, lying kicked back against the pillows, with his hand behind his head. She plopped down beside him when she finished. "What time are your parents coming up?"

Brent rolled on his side, propped up by an elbow. Before he replied to her question, he leaned over and kissed her. "Don't get mad, okay?"

Ruby sat cross-legged looking down at him. With a frown, she asked, "Get mad about what?"

"My parents aren't coming up. They drove to the Gulf with some friends." He glanced up and smiled at her and she scrambled swiftly off the bed.

Her face now flushed bright red. "You snake! You brought me up here under false pretenses. Don't think you'll be getting some, just because we're here by ourselves." She turned and left the bedroom, with Brent on her heels.

"Honey, I don't expect anything. I would have told you, but you wouldn't have come. It's the Fourth. I love being on the lake on the Fourth. Our dock has fireworks and a band plays music every night." Brent turned her gently around to face him. Ruby opened her mouth and then hesitated. Brent's hand brushed her cheek.

"Don't. You tricked me, Brent," she snapped. His eyes softened as he brushed her forehead with his lips. She had two choices: throw a fit and demand to be taken home, or try and have fun. He wouldn't take advantage of her, unless she wanted him to. Ruby knew she would have to control herself. He was devastatingly handsome and kissed like a dream. She blew out a deep breath. "You have to behave yourself and I mean it."

Brent gave her a serious look of longing for a silent moment and then said, "Ruby, I'm crazy about you. You have total control over me. I just want to make you happy. Besides, we won't be alone all weekend because tomorrow Reed is bringing up some new girl he's been dating. They're spending the night."

Brent knocked the breath out of her with that revelation. Reed had a date with a new girl, and if they were spending the night, Reed was probably screwing her, too. She didn't know why it bothered her so much, but it did.

"What happened to Reed and Tammy?" Ruby felt weak in the knees. She wanted to kick herself for asking the question the moment it escaped out of her mouth.

Brent's eyes darkened. Ruby had witnessed his volatile mood swings. He was mad. "Reed has never just dated Tammy. He goes out with different girls all of the time. Are you still holding out for Reed?"

Ruby punched him in the gut and walked outside to stand next to the rail, looking out at the night sky. He walked up behind her and pulled her to his chest. Ruby stiffened and gave him a mock elbow to the ribs. "You can be such a jerk sometimes. For your information, I could have had him if I wanted to, but I chose to go out with you instead."

He spun her around. "What? When?"

"The day after you first asked me out, he showed up at the store. Reed wanted me to go out with him the night of our first date. I turned him down." Well, technically she hadn't turned Reed down. He had left her there, kiss-swollen, in the parking lot of the store.

Brent picked her up in his arms and twirled her around. He kicked the sliding door opened and threw her on the bed. Brent was grinning from ear to ear. "You picked me over him, really?" She didn't have the heart to tell him she had kissed Reed, or the fact Reed's kisses still burned in her memory. It didn't matter; Reed wasn't hers. And Brent said he was crazy about her.

Brent snuggled against her neck and said in a voice as smooth as velvet, "Ruby, you're my fiery, redhead gal." His eyes had turned a dark emerald green with specks of gold, shimmering with passion, passion for her. Passion Reed didn't feel for her. Ruby quivered as Brent's hand ran down the front of her midriff. His mouth hungrily covered hers, and flames seared beneath her skin. This man wanted her.

BRENT WANTED HER, WANTED TO be inside of her, to taste her. To have her scream his name and tell him she loved him. Ruby was luscious and sweet, feisty and incredibly sexy. Brent couldn't care less about the *Tap It* game now. Ruby was the first woman he had ever dated who actually made him think about getting married, settling down and having a family.

He nipped her full bottom lip, gently tugging and sucking on it. She stared up at him with half-lidded eyes and her mouth parted. He drank her in, kissing her slowly and lazily to savor every second his mouth was connected to hers. Brent didn't try to ravish her as badly as he would have liked to. He wanted her to come to him willingly, begging even.

Brent felt Ruby melt beneath his touch, as little throaty moans escaped her lips. His hand held her possessively at her waist. "Make love to me, honey."

"No, I can't." Ruby moistened her lips and tried wiggling out of his arms, but he held her tightly.

"Make love to me or tell me why you can't." He nibbled her earlobe and then ran his tongue over her lips and into her mouth. His kiss was hot and demanding as she wrapped her arms around his neck. The stroke of his tongue was warm and inviting, the circling of their tongues became faster and deeper.

Ruby took a deep breath and replied, "Reed, I can't." Brent pulled her arms away from him and rose slowly to a sitting position and stared down at her. His expression was full of pain and rage. Ruby abruptly sat up and touched his face. "I'm so sorry, Brent. I have no idea why I said that. I don't know what to say."

Brent swung his legs away from her and sat on the edge of the bed. He cradled his face in his hands for a minute. Ruby placed a hand on his shoulder and he shoved her away and stalked out of the bedroom.

SHIT, SHIT, SHIT. WHAT IN the world had possessed her to call Brent, Reed? And at the very moment he asked her to make love to him. Geez, Louise. He was furious when he left the bedroom.

The den and the kitchen were both in the great room. Brent was at the stove cooking. She walked over and asked, "Can I help you with dinner?"

He didn't reply. Brent was giving her the ice treatment. It suddenly felt like the middle of winter, in July. Ruby turned and went back into the bedroom and put on her tennis shoes. She had to go run or walk, anything to get out of the cabin. If his mood hadn't changed by the time she returned, then she would ask him to take her home.

The night sky was lit by starlight. The summer wind was blowing hard as she ran down the winding driveway. Ruby could hear rustling in the woods and suddenly the music from *Deliverance* started playing in her mind. Geez, it was spooky out here. In the distance, she heard people from nearby cabins laughing and music playing in the background.

Ruby had run past the point when her side finally quit burning, and now her endorphins kicked in. Damn, why did Reed always have to creep into her thoughts and dreams? She was an idiot for calling Brent, Reed. Once she made it out to the highway, she stopped and bent over to catch her breath. Running felt good and she needed the release. Ruby reached in her pocket and held the amber stone. She thought about the drawing in the cave of the messenger holding the totem and heard a voice say, "Everything has a purpose and a time." Ruby wondered if it was just her imagination playing tricks on her. The stone warmed in her hand.

Headlights came down the driveway and the Camaro pulled to a stop beside her. Brent rolled down his window. "Get in the car, Ruby."

With curtness, she replied, "Brent, I prefer to walk or run back if you are going to be mad at me. I said I was sorry. You can take me home if you want to." Ruby stretched out her calf muscles and then her hamstrings. Another car rounded the curve honking and whistling at them. Ruby threw them a peace sign.

"Get in the damn car. I'm not going to ask you again." Brent was so mad his voice shook. Ruby watched as he gripped the steering wheel. She reluctantly got in the car and sat as far away from him as the car would allow.

"I'm not going to hurt you, woman. I have a right to be pissed. I'll get over it. It's funny, though; I never knew how this felt. I've done the same thing to other women before, but I've never had it done to me. Kudos, kid, you were born to play the game." Brent parked the car in the driveway and he strode back into the cabin, slamming the door behind him.

Ruby walked into the cabin and straight through the great room into the master bathroom. She reached in and turned on the shower. The bathroom walls were lined with old barn wood and the ceiling had been painted a dark, burnt orange. The sink and bathtub were copper, and the toilet had a pull string. The shower was all white with stainless steel heads. Ruby stepped in, allowing the hot water to run over her. She poured shampoo on her hand and washed her hair and then used her lavender soap and scrubbed her skin. Ruby dried off, and before opening the shower door, she wrapped her hair up in a towel.

Brent sat on the side of the bathtub when she stepped out of the shower. Ruby watched as he slowly raked his smoldering eyes over her. She quickly took the towel off her head and wrapped it around her body. "Good grief Brent, what are you doing in here?" A thunderbolt of shock shot through her.

He raggedly said, "God, you're so beautiful, all creamy and soft. I want to feel you next to me. I want you to love me, Ruby." Brent pulled her into his arms, crushing her against him, palming the back of her head. His kiss was demanding and intense, as he took complete possession of her mouth.

Brent knew how to kiss. He was a dang expert. He growled as he probed inside her mouth, one hand cupping her face and the other one at her waist. She felt his rock-hard erection pressed against her stomach.

Ruby knew she needed to stop kissing him or she wouldn't leave this room still a virgin. She just wanted a couple more of his hot, wet kisses. But Brent tugged at her towel, trying to dislodge it. She broke away from his kiss and pushed him off her, breathing hard.

"Don't you want me, Ruby?" He reached for her again and she threw up her hands to stop him.

Ruby had never thought it was anybody's business she was still a virgin at twenty. Most people her age had been actively engaging in sex since high school. Ruby wanted to choose who she gave herself to for the first time. She had the urge to laugh, but repressed it. "Brent, I do want you. But I'm not ready."

"Why?" Brent pleaded.

"If you must know, I'm still a virgin." Ruby wrapped the towel tighter around her as Brent stumbled back against the wall.

He shook his head back and forth in disbelief. "You're kidding." Ruby met his stare at eye level. "You're not kidding. Can I ask you a personal question and you give me an honest answer?"

He shoved one hand in his pocket and used the other to push his hair off his face.

"I strive to tell those I care about the truth, always. Would you mind if I get dressed first?" Ruby walked to the linen closet and grabbed another towel.

"Yes, I do mind. I want to know if Reed was the one standing here right now, would you tell him no?" Brent took a step closer to her. He searched her eyes, waiting for the truth.

"Reed isn't here. You're asking me a rhetorical question, but the answer would be the same. I want to give myself to the man I love, to the man who loves me, and who wants to marry me. I want the house and the picket fence, the two kids and the dog. That's what I want." Ruby shivered—not from the cold, but from the fact she didn't know if or when she would have the happily ever after in her life. She desired both Brent and Reed. But life just didn't work that way.

Brent picked up her hand and pulled it to his chest. He got down on one knee and she sucked in her breath. "Then marry me, Ruby Jane. I can give you all of those things and more." Ruby placed her hand on his face and then brushed the back of her fingers against the one-day stubble of his beard.

"Brent, I—I don't know what to say. I care for you, I do. I'm just not sure I'm in love with you. I don't want to hurt you, but you're moving way too fast for me. We only met a month ago." Ruby was suddenly very tired. She didn't want to hurt him. And if he were Reed, she would have made love to him. She stood up and walked to the vanity and began to brush the tangles out of her hair.

Brent walked up behind her and slanted his head down over her shoulder, pressing his lips against her neck. "I'll wait for you." And then, he left her alone.

RUBY DRIFTED OFF TO SLEEP in the master bedroom, alone. As she fell into a deep sleep, she dreamed of her wedding day. She stood at the entrance to the great room at Everglade Farms, surrounded by all her family and friends. The house was decorated for Christmas and the fire crackled in the fireplace. She felt an overwhelming sense of love as she walked the short distance across the room toward her groom. As he began to turn around, she awoke.

Ruby abruptly sat up in the bed, pulling the covers around her. She was still in Brent's grandfather's cabin. She got out of bed and reached down and picked up her shorts from the floor. Ruby pulled out the amber stone. She glanced over her shoulder to the clock on the nightstand. It was 5:00 a.m. and the sun would be up soon. She crawled back into bed, plumped up the pillow and closed her eyes. She would sleep for maybe another hour or so and then get up. Ruby fell back into a deep sleep, dreaming of the cave, flashes of stormy weather and people screaming.

AT EIGHT O'CLOCK, THERE WAS a knock on the cabin door. Brent opened the door and ushered in Reed and his new squeeze. He wanted to hate Reed. Brent wanted to punch his lights out, because Ruby had called him Reed. Instead, Brent said, "I have fresh coffee and pastries in the kitchen."

Brent caught Reed looking around for Ruby. "Ruby is still sleeping. Are you going to introduce your friend?"

Reed's expression lightened. "Sarah, this is Brent, one of my oldest friends in the 'boro. His grandparents own this place. Brent, Sarah and I work together at school." Sarah was a slight girl with raven hair and pale skin. She looked like a pretty porcelain doll—fragile.

Brent offered her his hand and a smile. "Sarah, it's nice to meet you. Make yourself at home, guys, while I go wake my girl." Brent noticed Reed's muscles tense when he said "my girl." *Hmm, so, Reed liked Ruby more than he was letting on.*

Brent knocked on the bedroom door and quietly entered the room. He walked over to the bed and looked down at Ruby. She was curled up in a ball with one hand around the pillow and the other one in a fist. He sat on the bed and brushed the hair off her face, tucking it behind her ear. He lowered his head and kissed her on the cheek. "Sleeping beauty, it's time to wake up."

Brent gently nudged her. "Wakey, wakey, eggs and bakey." Ruby rolled onto her back and her fist relaxed. She had been holding a piece of amber in her hand. He went to pick up the stone and she suddenly woke up.

Ruby looked at the stone and placed it quickly back into her pocket and then threw her arms around Brent's neck, holding on for dear life.

With a look of concern, he said, "What's this, honey? Did you have a bad dream?" Brent rubbed her back and she pressed her face into his chest.

"It was awful, terrible storms and tornadoes came up out of nowhere and a man was chasing me. Brent, I was so scared." She sniffled in Brent's arms while he stroked her hair.

"Honey, darling, it was just a dream. I'm here and you're here. Not a cloud in the sky. And I would kill any man who tried to harm one hair on your head." He lifted her chin and kissed her sweetly. He wanted to make her feel safe. He felt such protectiveness over her.

Brent scooped her up into his arms and carried her to the sliding glass doors. "See, it's awesome outside today. It's time to hit the water. You game? Reed and his friend Sarah are having coffee on the deck. Come on out when you're ready." He held her in his arms a moment longer, and as he started to let her down, she clung on to him. He said, "Sweetie, *that* was a bad dream. Wanna tell me about the rest of it? They can wait." She shook her head back and forth. He brought her over to the bed and they sat down.

Brent kissed her, brushing his lips softly over hers, then nibbled and tugged on her bottom lip before gliding his tongue over her teeth into her warm, wet mouth. His fingers twisted through her silky, auburn hair. He was in love with her. Win, lose or draw, nothing could change his feelings for her now. She could do whatever she wanted to him, as long as she stayed with him.

Ruby nipped his bottom lip and then he closed his mouth over hers hard, plunging his tongue into her depths. He was probably exploiting her vulnerability, but he couldn't help himself as she molded against his body. Brent wanted to devour her, crawl inside of her skin. He kissed her like he was making love to her mouth.

The image of her naked body from last night seared him, spurring him into a crazy frenzy, and he wanted to take from her whatever she would give. Brent skimmed his hand under her nightshirt and caressed her breast and she moaned. He began to lift her shirt over her head when he heard a knock on the sliding glass door.

"Damn it." Brent swore under his breath. He pulled her shirt down and turned to see Reed watching them.

"Get dressed, pumpkin. I guess they're getting anxious for the lake." If Brent had to guess, Reed wasn't anxious for the lake. Reed had been anxious to see what he and Ruby were doing in the bedroom—and it served Reed right for being a damn voyeur.

RUBY QUICKLY SHOWERED AND DRESSED for the lake. She wore a brightly colored string bikini under her blue-jean cutoffs and a Fleetwood Mac T-shirt. Ruby checked her beach bag to make sure she had her tanning oil, lip gloss, comb and sun visor. Ruby ran a brush through her hair, placed her shades on top of her head, and then walked into the great room.

Reed and his date were on the deck. *Weren't they cozy?* She had her arm around Reed's waist and he had his arm around her shoulders. Ruby narrowed her eyes and noticed Reed was kissing her dang ear. Reed's eyes met Ruby's and he smiled wickedly at her. Then he turned around and continued his assault on the new girl. *What a jerk!* She walked into the kitchen.

Ruby took a deep breath and pulled a coffee mug from the kitchen cabinet, poured her coffee and took a big gulp. Brent came in the back door with the cooler, sat it down in front of the fridge and said, "Give us a kiss and then help me with the cooler."

Ruby wrapped her arms around Brent's neck and he pulled her off the ground. He was in a good mood today, thank goodness! "You smell good, Brent."

He chuckled and opened the freezer door, grabbing the bag of ice, and then slammed it on the floor so loud she jumped.

"You scared the crap out of me. What else are we taking besides beer and sodas?" She pulled drinks out of the pantry and placed them inside the cooler.

"While you slept this morning, I put the ham, cheese and pickles in separate Glad bags. Grab the chips and bread out of the pantry. There's a brown paper bag on the bottom shelf." He packed the rest of the drinks while she grabbed the rest of the stuff.

Twenty minutes later, they were riding down the lake's channel, with the pontoon's nose rising slightly out of the water. The boat gently rocked over the waves as the breeze blew Ruby's hair. Brent was letting her drive the boat. He placed his hand on her shoulder and pointed. "When the channel splits, bear to the right."

Reed and Sarah sat in front of the boat. Ruby liked Sarah. She had an easygoing nature about her. But every time Reed touched her face or whispered in her ear, pain shot deep inside Ruby's chest.

Brent kissed her neck and asked, "You wanna ski back to the cove?"

What an outstanding idea! Skiing would keep her mind off Reed's flagrant seduction of Sarah. "Shoot, yeah!" Ruby replied.

Ruby and Brent swapped places at the helm and he brought the boat to a stop. Ruby pulled on her lifejacket and jumped into the water. Brent adjusted the ski boot and then shot it to her, making a sound like a gunshot echoing across the lake. She placed the boot on and pressed her heel down in the water to keep her balance. Then he shot her the second boot. Once she had the boots on, he threw her the ski rope and waited for her signal.

Ruby had the skis in place and the rope between her legs and yelled, "Boat driver!"

Brent slammed the boat's throttle down and took off. Ruby fought for a moment to keep her balance, and then she popped out of the water without falling once. With a jubilant cry, she yelled, "Woo hoo!" She brushed her hair out of her face with one hand and held onto the rope with the other. Ruby gave Brent the thumbs up, and then she remembered, the thumbs up sign meant to go faster.

Ruby readied herself for the jolt of speed and bent her knees slightly, leaning to the right, cresting over the waves. The water was a little choppy, but nothing she couldn't handle. She felt like she was flying. The pontoon soared across the channel to the cove.

In the cove, the water was like glass as Brent drove to the end and she gave him the thumbs down, letting go of the rope and slowly sinking down into the water. Ruby removed both skis as Brent circled back around to pick her up. She handed him the skis, and then he reeled in the rope.

Sarah ran and leaned over the back of the boat, grinning at Ruby. "Ruby, that was awesome! I've never been able to waterski. So cool, the way you jumped over the waves." Reed walked behind Sarah, pulling her back next to him.

Reed caught Ruby staring at him. A slow grin played across his lips as Ruby climbed back up the ladder. Her eyes were drawn to Reed's mouth, and she subconsciously wet her lips. Reed's eyes widened and Ruby noticed he clenched his teeth. Thankfully, Brent missed their exchange.

Brent pulled her into his arms and hugged her tightly. "You skied like a boss, woman!" He wrapped a beach towel around her and dried her off. Reed and Sarah returned to the front of the boat.

The pontoon had a deck on the back of the boat which allowed two people to lie out. Brent threw a couple of towels down and sat, motioning Ruby to join him. She lay on her stomach while Brent poured oil on his hands. He started working the oil into her shoulders, giving her a massage. A moan escaped her lips and she heard Reed ask Sarah to get in the water with him. A second later, Ruby heard splashes, but didn't move. Let Reed have his fun. She was having hers.

AFTER SECURING THE BOAT IN the slip at the dock, they drove back to the cabin. Ruby took a shower and finished dressing for the night and then walked into the den to wait on everyone else to get ready. Forty minutes later they headed out to listen to music and watch the fireworks at the dock. The little restaurant-turned-club was packed with people. The sheer size of Brent and Reed parted the sea of people and they found a table in the corner that offered a splendid view of the sunset. The band played a slow and sad tune from the Eagles. Several couples were dancing on the floor.

They ordered hamburgers and beers while Ruby ordered sweet tea. She would be the designated driver for the evening. As the evening wore on, the guys became drunk, which made Ruby and Sarah laugh so much they cried. The fireworks were fantastic. Brent held her in his arms and Reed held Sarah in his. Afterwards, Sarah grabbed her hand and they made their way to the restroom.

Inside, Ruby brushed her hair. Sarah was washing her hands when Ruby blurted out, "Do you like Reed?" Ruby didn't know if she really wanted the answer, but she needed to know.

Sarah glanced at her with a smirk. "Not the way you think. Reed's not really my type." Sarah dried her hands with the paper towels.

Ruby applied her coral-colored lipstick and then turned toward Sarah, not quite believing her ears. "How in the world is Reed Jackson not your type?" Ruby moved against the wall, so the two other girls who had just walked in could use the mirror. Sarah grabbed Ruby's hand and they walked outside onto the sidewalk.

"Sit down for a second. Let's make them sweat for a little while." Ruby sat down beside her on the pier's sidewalk. "Reed's not my type, because you are." Ruby's eyes got as big as silver dollars when the realization struck her.

"Holy shit! Does Reed know?" Sarah laughed so hard she snorted, which made Ruby laugh with her. A Tanya Tucker song wafted through the air as people walked by them. They rocked their legs back and forth over the water.

"Yes, Reed knows, sweet thang. He brought me up here today to make you jealous. I'll kill you, if you tell him I told you that." Sarah pulled a cigarette out of her purse and lit it, taking a slow drag.

Ruby smiled. She couldn't help it. Reed wanted to make her jealous. "Well, it worked! I've been jealous all day." They both laughed again, holding onto their sides.

Sarah's expression turned serious. "I have no idea what's going on between the three of y'all, but it's freaking me out. It's like there's all this sexual heat and energy building up here and it's directed toward you. Reed is really a nice guy and I generally love him."

Ruby explained the *Tap It* game to Sarah. Sarah listened, occasionally shaking her head. Thirty minutes must have passed before Ruby finished unloading all of her feelings and emotions to this virtual stranger. "So, I'm in a 'damned if I do, damned if I don't' situation."

"Wow. I mean, wow. For what it's worth, Reed may not know it, but he's in love with you. I know Brent is in love. He's ate up with it. Somebody's going to get really hurt. I just hope it isn't you." Before

Sarah got up, she kissed Ruby. Ruby's mouth dropped open after Sarah pulled away and formed an O.

On the way back into the restaurant, they met Brent and Reed. Ruby must have looked pale because Brent said, "Honey, did you get sick? You're pale as a ghost." Ruby nodded yes. She was sick of the damn game. She was stunned by Sarah's kiss. Ruby suddenly wanted to be at Everglade Farms, safe and sound from the whole lot of them.

AFTER THE FOURTH OF JULY, Brent's possessiveness and jealousy were starting to really annoy Ruby. She had enjoyed his company, for the most part, but she hated it when his temper flared. Ruby could totally forget about talking to anyone of the opposite sex. She could have grown to love him, but Ruby hated he was so jealous.

Brent had stopped by the store one night to take her to dinner.

Rusty, an old high school friend, had stopped in to pick up a few groceries. He had leaned on the counter on his forearms. "You should've seen it RJ. Sandy and I were riding down by the river when her horse took off and bucked her off, right in the water. She was so mad she kicked the horse in the behind. I laughed so hard I cried. That Sandy, man, she is all woman."

Ruby was laughing so hard tears were streaming down her face. "Oh, Rusty, I wish I had been there. I haven't been riding all summer."

Rusty grabbed his bags and said, "I'll take you next time." That's when she looked up to find Brent standing there with steam practically coming out of his ears.

"Check ya later, RJ." Rusty turned and gave Brent a look that said "Come on, big boy, if you think you're big enough to handle me."

Ruby wiped down the counter. "What's wrong? Why are you mad, now?"

Brent looked back out the store door and walked over to Ruby. No one was in the store except the two of them. "Who the hell was that?"

"Are you for real? Geez Louise, I went to high school with him, and he's going out with Sandy. You can't expect me to work at the store and not talk to people. What happened to you to make you so jealous? Ah, I get it now. You don't trust yourself, so you're not going to trust me." Ruby hit her mark. Brent wasn't the faithful type, but she had known that about him before she started dating him.

He walked back to the freezer section and grabbed a strawberry shortcake ice cream bar. At the counter, he began to tease her. "I'm a customer now. Wanna flirt with me?"

Ruby rolled her eyes at him. "You and I will never work if you keep up this attitude of yours. Your jealousy is suffocating me to death."

"I can't help it. I'm jealous because I desire you. I want you. That guy, he was flirting with you, and you looked like you were enjoying it." Brent took a bite out of his ice cream.

It was useless for Ruby to talk to him when he got mad. He was too darn stubborn. "Good grief, you're hopeless. I'm sorry, but I can't go to dinner tonight. Mama's canning tomatoes and I told her I would help her when I got off work." Her mother had been canning, but she was likely through by now. Ruby just didn't want to be with Brent.

His expression softened. "I can help y'all can tomatoes."

Ruby really wanted him to go back to town. "You don't have to. Call me tomorrow, and we'll figure out something for the weekend. I have to close the register and lock up."

"I believe you're trying to get rid of me." He took another bite of his ice cream and closed his eyes. "This ice cream is good stuff."

She shook her head and chuckled. He looked like a little boy. "You're really too much. Meet me on the store porch."

He offered her a bite and she took it. Brent stepped outside on the porch and sat in one of the big rockers while he waited for Ruby to close.

Ruby closed the store and locked the door. Brent rocked in the chair and said, "It's really nice out here. You still want me to go home?"

He followed her to her car, and she opened the door. "To be honest, I just need some 'me' time, okay?" She kissed him lightly.

"You are the only girl I've ever dated who brushes me off. I think I'm becoming a glutton for punishment. I'll call you tomorrow."

He tried to start kissing her, but she pushed him away. "Brent, I'm tired. I'll talk to you, later." Ruby jumped in her car and left before he could put up a fight. She could swear, the harder she pushed him away, the harder he tried to stay with her.

Chapter 6

If I Were Your Woman

RUBY AND BRENT WOULD OCCASIONALLY double-date with Reed and Tammy, now she and Reed had called a sort of truce. Sarah had told Reed about kissing Ruby. He had later apologized to Ruby for trying to make her jealous. She still loved Reed's sense of humor and laughter. She was still crazy about him. Reed seemed to act different around Tammy. He was polite to her, but Ruby didn't see any sparks of passion. Not like the night he had kissed her. That night seemed so long ago; it had been at the first of summer, and now July was coming to an end.

Brent and Ruby had planned an outing with Reed and Tammy to Opryland USA on the last Friday in July. Opryland had opened only five years earlier and Ruby loved to go every summer. Her favorite rides were the roller coasters, like the Timber Topper. More recently, they had added the Wabash Cannonball. The day had started out great. They watched several of the music shows and rode the thrill rides.

They came off the Flume Zoom log ride, soaking wet. It felt great to cool off on a sweltering ninety-degree day in Tennessee. Brent pulled Ruby up in his arms and then pinched his nose and teasingly said, "Whew, you smell like a fish."

Ruby promptly puffed out her cheeks, pursed her lips, and placed her hands behind her ears, imitating a blowfish. She walked around them with the distorted face and when she saw a couple of older people, she made the face at them, too. Everyone laughed at Ruby's silly antics.

Brent ran over to a lemonade stand and ordered a couple of drinks to go. He handed one glass to Ruby and the other lemonade to Tammy. He picked up Ruby and twirled her around saying, "I love you, Ruby Jane Glenn."

Ruby peered over her shoulder to see Reed's reaction, but he and Tammy had walked away to give them privacy. Reed didn't give a crap about her. She had been delusional earlier in the summer when he had kissed her.

Ruby let out a sigh. Brent cared for her. She just didn't think he really loved her. "Brent, do you really love me? Or is this just the final part of *Tap It*. I tell you 'I love you,' and you win. Or I don't tell you, and I win. Is that it?"

Brent reached up and touched the side of her face. "I do love you more than anyone I've ever known. I want you to be with me, always. You win *Tap It*, Ruby Jane. I profess my undying love to you."

Ruby couldn't breathe and began to panic. This was why she hated dating. Someone in a relationship always hurts the other one. She wasn't in love with Brent. The game was over. She had won. "Brent, I don't know what you want me to say. I love being with you. I really do. But, I'm not in love with you."

The pain reflected in Brent's eyes was there because of her. She hated herself for it. Brent pleaded with her, "Please don't say that. You don't mean it."

Brent wrapped his arms tightly around her. The embrace should have been comforting, but it wasn't, because there was one more important caveat in the equation: Reed. It wasn't fair to Brent, and she knew she had to put an end to their relationship. This whole *Tap It* scene had finally played out and she was finished.

"Brent, I don't think we need to keep seeing each other. It's not fair to you, and it's not fair to me. You need someone who can give you what you want. I can't."

Brent began to fume. He took the drink out of her hand and just threw it. God help anyone in its path.

Ruby constantly walked on eggshells around him. Brent got mad when she worked in the store, when she went out with Anna and Sandy. Hell, she was afraid to sit on the pot without asking him first.

Brent grabbed her shoulders. His face darkened and he looked downright dangerous. His voice was cold as ice. "That's a damn guy's line, Ruby. You can't or you won't? Damn it, why do you always have to push me away? Do you have any idea how many women wish they could be in your shoes right now?"

Brent's arrogance over his handsome looks, and his need to remind her of it, made Ruby see red. "Oh, good grief! Why don't you go after one of them, then, and leave me alone?" She started to storm off.

Brent reached out, placing his hand on her forearm. "Stop it. Ruby! I don't want to fight with you. Let's just cool it and enjoy what we have left of the day. We can talk about this later. Come on. Reed and Tammy keep looking at us."

Brent touched her shoulder and she brushed it away. By the time she reached Reed and Tammy, she was madder than a wet hen. Ruby pushed her thoughts away from Brent and listened to the music as it filled the air. The Tin Lizzie ride had a line of kids as she passed by it. Ruby had finally calmed down by the time they reached the entrance to the Wabash Cannonball.

Tammy pouted and crossed her arms defiantly as she tilted her head to view the massive roller coaster. "There is no way I'm getting on that ride! It turns upside down. I'll be sick."

Reed rubbed Tammy's arm. "You don't have to. But I've been dying to ride this thing all year. Will you be okay if I go with Brent and Ruby?"

Brent and Ruby continued to glare at each other. He shot a look to Reed and said, "I'll stay with Tammy. You and Ruby go ahead."

The line to the Wabash was very long and screams echoed from the riders as the ride swooshed along the rails. Ruby could feel the vibrations of the roller coaster under her feet. Once they were out of earshot from Brent and Tammy, Reed said, "Ruby, what's wrong? Did y'all have a fight?"

Ruby gazed into Reed's eyes. She had a major crush on the man standing so close to her now. A fiery jolt of energy surged between them. She looked into the unfathomable depths of his eyes and was forever lost.

The crowd in line pushed them forward and Ruby nearly fell, when Reed caught her. "You okay, princess?" He quickly let her go; his simple touch made her pulse race.

"Yes, I'm fine," Ruby blurted out. "Reed, do you love Tammy?" Well, she'd done it now.

Reed smoothed the hair from her eyes. "I care about Tammy. But if you're asking me if I'm in love with Tammy, I'm not. I've been waiting on you, Ruby. I've been waiting on you to be through with Brent and that damn game."

Ruby's eyes filled with tears, while her voice shook with fury. "Why have you waited nearly all summer to tell me that? *Reed*, you've been making out with Ms. Priss! And I've been with Brent all summer. You should have said something instead of acting like my best friend."

Reed took a step away from her. With a lazy smile, he said, "You were the one who wanted to play *Tap It*. Let's not forget that, please."

Ruby punched him in the arm, and he said, "Ow. Look it's our turn." He held out his hand and she grabbed it as they boarded the ride. Their bodies were pressed tightly together in the ride's seat as the gate sealed shut.

Ruby didn't know whether to be pissed at him or ecstatically happy. Reed had just confessed he didn't love Tammy. She kept her feelings in check. She didn't know if what he said was really true, but Ruby did know she was crazy gaga over him.

As the ride began to rock out of the station, they began a seventy-foot climb and then dipped into an utterly scary U-turn toward the first major plunge. It felt like they were suspended in time. They looked at each other, laughing, and then they both began to scream. The roller coaster approached the double corkscrew flip and their eyes were wide with excitement, and then they screamed and laughed some more.

When the ride came to an end, Reed helped her out. Her legs were wobbly as he put his arms around her. She closed her eyes only for a second to savor the feeling and then looked up into his eyes.

Reed bent over to kiss her, but she pulled away. "No, don't. Not yet. You have a date with Tammy and I'm with Brent. We'll have to pick this up later."

He pressed his face to her cheek and whispered in her ear, "Meet me tonight, Ruby. Come to my apartment at eight."

Her expression was excited, but hesitant. "I can't come to your apartment. What if Brent came over and found me there?" Ruby walked with Reed through the exit gate. Reed filled her with a roller coaster of emotions, and wow, what a ride!

"You broke up with him?" Reed asked as he held her hand a little while longer.

She replied reluctantly, "Well, not technically, but I am, tonight. I don't want to hurt him. Come to Everglade Farms. Do you know where I live?" Ruby's hands were tingling.

He stopped her before they were in full view of Brent and Tammy. "Yes, I know where you live."

Her eyes searched his as she said, "Down the street from my house there is an old abandoned church and cemetery that sits on top of a hill. There is a driveway that goes around the back of the place. Meet me there around eight o'clock.

He pulled her into his arms once more before letting her go. "Okay, I'll be there."

RUBY TRIED HARD NOT TO look at Reed on the drive back from Nashville, for fear Brent would know the truth from her face. Ruby was in love with Reed. She hated to hurt Brent, but there was no other way around it. Brent and Ruby didn't talk much until they dropped off Reed and Tammy. She was trying to formulate exactly what she would say to him. Brent had one hand on the wheel when he reached over with the other to hold her hand.

Ruby moved her hands to her lap. "Brent, it's no use. I'm sorry but I'm not in love with you. I don't want to hurt you."

Brent gripped the steering wheel with both hands and pressed on the accelerator. He rushed through the traffic lanes, dodging in and out of cars, driving like a mad man.

Ruby buckled her seatbelt and twisted around in her seat to see him nearly crash into a semi truck. She covered her eyes and screamed, "Slow down. What are you trying to do, kill us?"

Brent let up on the gas and checked his side and rearview mirrors before moving into the slow lane. "You're delusional if you think Reed's in love with you."

Ruby sucked in a breath and stared at him, unsure what to say next. "What do you mean?' She fidgeted in the seat and dug in her purse for the amber stone and she held it in her hand.

Brent glanced to her and then back at the road. "I'm not a fool! You've been pining after him all summer. It's really kind of pathetic." Brent's words stung her. Dazedly, she wondered if Brent had known all along about her feelings for Reed. Why hadn't he dumped her? Part of her wanted to take her fingernails and gouge his eyes out, while the other part wanted to feel sorry for him.

Ruby steeled herself, and after a moment said, "You're trying to hurt me, and I don't blame you. I'm sorry."

He retorted, "You're the one who is going to be sorry. You think the game is over, don't you?" He honked the horn at a car that pulled out in front of them. "Get out of the damn way."

Brent shot her a brief glare as he continued to lash out. "The game is over between you and me, sweetheart, not you and Reed. That game is just starting. I can tell you from experience Reed never loses, ever. You seem to forget, I've watch Reed play this game for three years. And in three years, I've only won once. You've gotten it in your pretty little head that Reed's the good guy and I'm the bad one. Well, we're both bad, honey."

Brent's breathing became labored and the muscles in his biceps were so tight that they threatened to rip his skin apart. He said, "Don't be stupid. Did he ever tell you he wasn't playing the game, Ruby?"

Ruby stared out the window as they passed the scenic vistas along Highway 99. Her mind raced back and forth between what Reed had said earlier in the park and what Brent was saying now in the car. Brent's pride was hurt, and his unmitigated arrogance was starting to piss her off. "Reed said his feelings for me weren't part of the game." Ruby nervously began to bite the edge of the skin next to her fingernail.

The muscles in Brent's jaw were clenched tightly when they turned onto Morgan Road. He said through gritted teeth, "But he never said he wasn't going to play, did he?"

Ruby turned white as a sheet. She couldn't say anything, because Brent was right.

Brent's expression softened. He placed his hand on her thigh and said softly, "Poor, sweet Ruby, you're in love with the wrong man.

Don't you think you could grow to love me? I'm crazy about you. I want you to be the mother of my children. I want to grow old with you."

Holy shit, Brent was losing his freaking mind. She pushed his hand away and continued staring out the window. She had been a fool to think someone as gorgeous as Reed would fall for someone like her.

Brent turned his right blinker on and pulled down a tractor lane and stopped his car. He turned to face her. "Is he the reason you never made love to me? Tell me the truth."

She whipped her head around and in a fit of fury said, "I've never lied to you, not once!"

"Then tell me the truth now," he said.

Tears sprang to her eyes and spilled down her cheeks. "Yes, he is the reason. Are you happy now?"

With sadness, Brent replied, "No, I'm not happy, not at all. I just wish you would really give me a chance, once you see the real truth about him."

She crossed her arms, holding herself. Full of anger and disillusionment, Ruby said, "I'm through with *Tap It*. I thought I could compete and maybe teach you both a lesson. Instead, I taught myself one. Never date players. I don't want to see you anymore." She didn't want to see either of them again. *Tap It* had taken its toll on her.

Brent flinched and reached over to pull Ruby into his arms, but she pushed him away. "You don't mean it; you're just upset."

"You're damn right I'm upset. I have nothing left to say." Ruby held the door handle as Brent started his car and drove the short distance to Everglade Farms. Ruby jumped out quickly when the car stopped. Brent ran and caught her by the hand before she could run inside.

Max trotted down the sidewalk and tried to lick Brent's hand. He shooed Max away and touched the side of her arm. Brent pleaded with Ruby, "Don't leave me. Don't do this to us."

She looked at his hand on her arm and then back up to his eyes. Ruby wanted to send him away so he would never come back. Ruby jerked her arm away. "I'm sure you'll find a replacement before the night ends."

Brent crushed her into his arms, holding her tightly. "I'm not going to be able to stop loving you, just because you don't want to see me."

She felt the pounding in his chest. Her hands trembled as she pushed him away. "Goodbye, Brent." She ran up the porch steps and into the house.

RUBY WATCHED FROM HER WINDOW as Brent slowly pulled out of her driveway. She felt a heavy weight in her chest. Brent's words had cut her to the core. Now, she wondered if they were true.

Ruby walked down the hall and into the bathroom. She pushed back the shower curtain and reached down to turn on the faucet. Ruby stripped down and stepped inside, leaning her head back under the streaming water. For a few minutes, she allowed the hot water to run over her, easing the tension across her shoulder blades. She was preparing herself for battle; if Reed was playing her, it would end tonight.

After her shower, Ruby made her way into her bedroom and closed the door. She sat in front of her dresser and intended to use everything in her arsenal to make herself at least feel pretty. She applied foundation, eye shadow, eyeliner and mascara. She curled her hair quickly with a curling iron.

Ruby opened her closet door, moving through the rack of clothes until she came across her teal spaghetti strap top and paired it with her khaki shorts and then slipped on her sandals. Ruby dabbed Halston behind her earlobes and between her breasts. Finally, she added coral lipstick, which brought out the fullness of her lips.

Ruby was running down the steps toward the front door when her mom walked out of the den to meet her. Lee looked at Ruby with eyes full of concern. "My, honey, you look beautiful tonight, but I thought Brent just left." How did her mother always know when she was hurting?

Ruby looked at her mom, nearly on the brink of tears. "Mom, we broke up. I'm meeting Reed."

Her mom had a confused look on her face. Lee asked, "Brent's friend, Reed?"

"Yes, Mom. I have to go. We'll talk later." Ruby kissed her and dashed out the door. Her mom didn't have a clue Ruby had been playing that stupid dating game.

Ruby could have walked up the hill to the church, but decided to drive. She had no plan, no thought-out words. She just wanted the game over, once and for all.

Chapter 7

Take It To The Limit

RUBY WATCHED REED PULL HIS car up the hill and park behind hers. She was sitting on one of the Campbells' tombstones. He walked to her car and looked inside. Reed looked so good in his white shorts and yellow button-down shirt, which he had rolled up to his elbows. He turned and spotted her. He waved, breaking into a grin that would have melted butter.

"Hey, whatcha doing sitting in the graveyard?" He walked over and sat on the edge with her.

Ruby raised one shoulder and said softly, "Talking to the dead." The night was hot and sticky as she combed her fingers through her hair, allowing the small breeze to hit her neck. She could smell Reed's masculine scent mixed with Aramis cologne. He was all man, nothing but hard-as-a-rock steel. He made her weak in mind and body. She tried hard to focus on the task at hand.

Reed's lighthearted expression changed quickly when he looked at her. His jaw actually dropped open. "God, you're so beautiful."

Ruby came close to laughing, seeing the surprised expression on his face. She met his gaze. "Yeah, well, not as pretty as you are."

Reed tensed hearing the edge in her voice. His hand cupped her chin and lifted her face to his. "What's the matter?"

"Brent said I was a fool for being in love with you. That *Tap It* was just starting between you and me. He said you never lose. Is it true?" His eyes bored into hers as though he could read her deepest, darkest secrets. Her skin heated from the look Reed gave her.

His brows creased with concern. "I told you I wasn't playing the game, Ruby. Are we going back there?"

"Do you love me, Reed?" Ruby wanted him to tell her the truth. If he didn't, then she would let him go and try to build a life where he wouldn't be a part of it. It seemed impossible that only a couple of months ago her life had been normal. She would never be normal again. He had changed that for her.

Reed managed to croak out an answer. "I'm not sure what love is, Ruby. All I know is I can't stop thinking about you."

Ruby listened to his cop-out answer. She had fallen for Reed all summer. As their friendship deepened over the last few weeks, she knew she was lost in love and had made Brent suffer for it. She felt guilty over Brent and confused over her feelings for Reed.

She needed to know if the signals Reed had been sending her were valid. "You can't stop thinking about me? You don't know what love is? Well, I will tell you what love means to me. It may not be the Webster definition of love, but I know what love feels like. I know when I'm around you, my moods change, my temperature spikes, and my ability to think straight goes out the window. Being near you makes me happy and sad. Sometimes you make me sick. But I would rather have my feelings for you, than to never have had them at all."

The breeze rustled in the pine and cedar trees and she pushed the hair off her face. "Riddle me this, if you can't stop thinking about me, why did you let me stay with Brent all summer?"

Reed let out an exasperated sigh. He looked up into the sky like he was praying for deliverance and then he looked back down to her. "I've felt all of those emotions. You have driven me crazy this summer. I haven't been able to eat or sleep. I have followed you and Brent around all summer, just to be near you. When I looked into your bedroom at the lake and saw Brent pulling your shirt off, I was insane with jealousy. I wanted to kill both of you. I talked my coworker into coming with me to the lake, just so I could be near you. Even if it meant I had to watch you in his arms and see him kiss you. I thought you were playing *Tap It*. But that morning, you had desire in your eyes for Brent, not me."

Ruby leaned closer to him. The power between them was like a magnet to steel. Her voice quivered between anger and tears. "You could have put a stop to Brent and me weeks ago. The night you kissed me, you could have asked me not to go out with him. You didn't fight for me once! Instead, you let me remain in the arms of another, while you continued to have sex with Ms. Priss."

Reed threw his hands up in the air and then pulled her up to him. "Good god, Ruby! Why are you doing this now? We can finally be together, and you're trying to sabotage us."

Ruby stood toe-to-toe with him, her hands balled up in fists. Her anger rose to the point of no return. "Me, sabotage us? You knew about the game the whole damn time. You knew the night at the store and the ballgame. You were a damn coward not to tell me or stop it before it even started. I think you were playing the game the whole time. I'm not a fool, I'm not!"

Reed's hands dropped away and he paced back and forth and then stopped to face her. "I wasn't playing the game! I told you! That night at the store, I came to ask you out. What did you want me to do? You never called me, remember? You were supposed to call me when you were through with the game and Brent. Did you forget that?"

Ruby shook while she shouted at him. "I don't call guys! I don't intend to start now. I'm finished with *Tap It*. I don't want any more games. Go on back to Tammy or god knows who else you have waiting in the wings." She spun around and headed to her car, but Reed caught her, turning her around to face him.

Ruby felt Reed's fingers tremble as he spoke in a low and dangerous voice. "I can't believe what I'm hearing. You do realize you're doing exactly what Brent wants you to do. He doesn't want you with me. I couldn't fight for you. You had to leave him first."

Ruby opened her hands, palms up, and shrugged. "See, I don't get it. You and Brent have played this game for three years. You didn't care what Brent thought about the other girls. You went after them. You didn't even try to come for me, not once." Tears sprang into her eyes.

Reed let go of her and took a step back. "This isn't about Brent or what he thinks. It was about you and what you wanted. Yeah, we had stolen glances this summer, but you never indicated you really wanted me. Not one time, not until today. I didn't come after you, damn it, because I thought you were in love with Brent."

Ruby's shoulders slumped and she closed her eyes for a moment. She opened them to look into his eyes. "I'm tired and confused."

Reed's lips brushed softly against her cheek. He whispered, "Then believe me, Ruby. Give me a chance."

Her head fell forward to rest on his shoulder. "I really want to believe you. I'm in love with you," she said, gravely. "I see the same sky above me, the same stars and moon, but nothing will ever be the same for me, because I love you." Whoever said love was grand evidently had never been in love. This sucked. Ruby pulled back from him slightly and cradled his face in her hands while she searched his eyes. "There, I have professed my love to you, the game is over. You have won."

He said, "Silly goose, I told you this thing between us has nothing to do with *Tap It*." He scooped her up in his arms. His mouth crushed over hers. His kiss was raw and demanding. He probed inside her mouth with his hot, wet tongue, plunging in and out, gliding over her teeth. He adjusted his angle and then he devoured her. Reed twisted his fingers in her hair, pulling her closer to him. The world could end right this very minute and she didn't care. Reed was kissing her, sweeping her away into a state of euphoria.

Ruby had been waiting on Reed her whole life. She knew she was way out of her depth, but she didn't care as long as he kept kissing her. He pulled and sucked on her lower lip and then nibbled her top one. His mouth covered hers and his expert tongue made her want more than just kissing. She wanted every bit of him. Reed pushed her back against the car and grabbed the strap of her top, pushing it over her shoulder to give him access to her breast.

Ruby broke from his kiss for a moment to breathe. She couldn't think. She needed oxygen. Reed hadn't professed love to her, but maybe he cared for her. Ruby tilted her head back and gazed into the dark, burnished color of his eyes, the quirk of his sideways grin, so invitingly kissable. The man was simply too gorgeous for words and she was helplessly lost.

Reed said in a sexy Southern drawl, "Ruby, you know there are really no guarantees in this life. All I can tell you is, while we are together, I will cherish you."

Resigning to whatever he was offering her, she sighed. "I don't expect anything from you." Ruby knew she was setting herself up for a whole world of hurt loving him. Her blood pounded in her veins as she tried to wiggle out of his arms.

Reed held her tighter, with one arm around her waist as he tilted her chin up to him. She trembled under his touch and melted under his glare. "You should expect everything. You should want everything. That's what you deserve." The heat intensified between them. Ruby felt flushed and restless. She wanted him but knew in the end he would crush her. There would be no pieces left to pick up. Ruby knew she should tear herself from his arms. She should stand up to him and tell him to "kiss it where the sun doesn't shine."

But she didn't, and she never broke eye contact. Her voice quivered. "Take me, Reed, eat me up, and spit me out." Ruby laid her hand on his cheek. "Come with me." Then she caught his hand and led him to the passenger side of her car and opened the door. Ruby entered the back seat. She lay back as he stretched his body over hers. The sultry look on his face made her want to strip naked. His muscular body molded against the softness of hers. Reed's tongue glided over her lips and into her mouth. His warm breath mingled with hers as little shallow gasps escaped from her. She tingled everywhere Reed touched. His scrumptious smell clouded her brain. Women threw themselves at Reed, and here he was, with her.

He moaned when he kissed her, as Ruby trailed her fingers along the solid muscles of his arms. He adjusted his body slightly to have more room and she felt the hardness of his arousal pressed against her and couldn't resist arching her back in response.

"Sugar, you're so sweet." He nuzzled against her neck and then gently bit the bottom of her earlobe. When he placed his tongue inside her ear, she practically convulsed underneath him. His hands slowly went around to cup her bottom and her thighs scissored between his. He ran his hand up her leg toward the edge of her shorts and his fingers slipped inside her panties. His fingers pressed against her soft delicate skin and she nearly came on the spot.

"I want to taste you, Ruby." His voice dripped with honey as he began to pull her top off, and she stilled his hands.

Razor sharp desire clutched her insides making her tummy flutter. "Reed, as much as I want to make love to you, I'm not ready."

"Hmm, point taken. It may not happen tonight, but, Ruby, I am going to make love to you." His words made her want to faint. She felt light-headed and dizzy. He reached up to touch her face and then angled his head to press light, feathery kisses along her neck. He murmured, the words vibrating against her neck, "I won't make love to you, honey, not until you tell me to."

The high beams of a car pulled up behind Reed's car and stopped. Then Ruby saw the blue lights. "Shit, shit! Get up, Reed, the sheriff's here." Ruby scrambled quickly to adjust her clothing and opened the car door. She walked back to meet the sheriff's deputy. She couldn't tell who was working tonight, because a flashlight was shining in her eyes.

"Ruby Glenn, is that you, young'un? I didn't see your car." Deputy Gilley turned off his flashlight and crossed the driveway to meet her.

"Hey, Dan, I'm sorry. I needed some privacy and I thought this place would do the trick." She shoved her hands in her pockets and heard Dan chuckle.

"Yeah, privacy, right, Ruby. Y'all need to move along. I had a call come in and wanted to make sure no one was up here vandalizing the cemetery. Tell your mama I said hello." Deputy Dan turned and made his way back to the sheriff's car, turned off the blues and backed down the driveway.

Ruby sighed and felt Reed's warm breath on her neck as he pressed a kiss on her skin, so light and feathery chills ran up her spine. Her head fell back against his shoulder. It couldn't be wrong to need Reed's touch. She longed for his touch. Ruby wanted to give herself to him, physically and emotionally. Ruby longed to feel like a woman and experience the rush of pleasure that came with making love to a man. Deputy Dan probably saved her from losing her virginity in the backseat of her car tonight.

REED AND RUBY LINGERED BY the driver side of her car watching the deputy pull down the long driveway. Reed sizzled from the touch of her skin. She had yielded, opening herself and inviting him to take more. And he wanted more, much more. Ruby smelled of the summer sun and wildflowers. Her skin was so soft, like velvet. Ruby had overwhelmed him with emotions. Reed stepped away from her.

Ruby blinked and shook her head. She stammered, "Why did you stop kissing me?"

"Ruby," he said in a different tone. "I won't make you promises I can't keep." He looked at her with a pained expression. He was fighting hard not to show he desired her.

"I don't want to hurt you. I..." He stopped speaking. Reed was fighting himself, an inner struggle—he wanted to make love to her, but he was falling in love with her.

"I'm a big girl, Reed. I can take care of myself." She took a deep breath. "I guess that's enough kissing for one night, anyway."

He laughed. "You think?" He linked his fingers with hers.

Ruby's brown, doe eyes were wide and offered him a promise of love. "Yeah, this isn't a sprint, it's a marathon."

Reed's head fell back in laughter. But when his fingers ran across her silky skin, all he could think about was how good she would feel with him deep inside her, sending a wave of desire crashing over him. She was pretty damn sexy too. He had dated plenty of women, but Ruby was different. He actually liked her and enjoyed her company. They were friends. They laughed at the same jokes and loved the same music. He would take his time with her. He wanted this, whatever this was, to last longer than his typical tryst. He had cut it off with Tammy when Brent dropped them off today. Tammy had cried, but she didn't love him. Tammy only liked having Reed as her eye candy to flaunt in front of her friends.

Ruby had told him tonight she loved him. He knew she meant it, he could feel it, too. That made the stakes higher for both of them. He cocked his head to the side and said, "So, you wanna go out with me?"

Ruby jumped up, wrapped her arms around his neck and gave him a big kiss. She lifted a brow and said, "What do you think?"

Reed held her in his arms with his fingers cupped under her ass. He gave her a devilish smile and said, "I think I'm going to regret ever meeting you, Ruby Jane." And then he hugged her tightly.

Ruby tried wrestling out of his grip. She furrowed her brow. "What the heck?"

He picked her up and sat her down on the top of her car hood and then touched the tip of her nose with his finger. "You're trouble, with a capital T."

She slid down off her car and pushed him away, playfully. She pointed to the cemetery and said, "Digging yourself a grave here, Reed, and I don't have to go far to bury you."

The moon and the stars were out now, and insects could be heard rustling in the grass around them. The scent of pine and cedar mixed with the old rosebushes planted around the gate to the cemetery filled the air.

Ruby smiled up to him. "I have to work until eight o'clock tomorrow night and then I'm meeting Anna and Sandy at Ditch Lane. Why don't you meet me there?"

There was a wild man inside of him when Ruby's curves were pressed against him. Reed grabbed her by her buttocks. "Oh, I plan on showing up. I plan on being your shadow. I don't want you out of my sight." Ruby kissed him senseless again.

RUBY PUSHED AWAY FROM HIM before she lost her head again. Her mouth had gone bone-dry feeling him next to her. She rested her hand on his chest and gazed up into his dark eyes framed by those gorgeous lashes. "I need to go. I have to get up early to help Mom in the garden, before I go to work. I need my beauty sleep."

He playfully added, "Honey, you don't need any beauty sleep. You're so pretty you could stay up all night." Reed kissed her one more time and then walked to his car. Before he stepped inside, he tossed her one last glance. Reed started his car, blinked his headlights at her and then backed out of the driveway.

Ruby drove up the driveway to her home. She had planned on ending her relationship with Reed before it had started. It was funny how life decided those things for you. She entered the house quietly. Everyone was in bed. Ruby locked the doors and climbed the stairs to her bedroom. She washed her face, brushed her teeth and combed her hair out before slipping on an oversized T-shirt to sleep in. She slipped between the cool, clean cotton sheets and ruffled her pillow next to her cheek. As she closed her eyes, she could see Reed's beautiful face. She would have good dreams tonight.

THE NEXT NIGHT, RUBY ARRIVED at one of the last summer parties of the year. Everyone she knew was at Ditch Lane. She was working her way through the crowd toward the bonfire, talking and laughing with different people, when Jerry came up behind her and grabbed her bum like he had done at least a thousand times before.

"Hey, sweet pea, what's up? No Brent tonight?" He gave her a questioning look. It was weird how easily Jerry could read her sometimes.

"Nope, I broke up with him yesterday." She linked her arm through his and walked to the bonfire to meet up with Sandy and Anna.

Jerry grabbed Anna's bum next, and she squealed with delight. He said, "Ruby broke up with Brent."

Sandy turned to face her. Ruby shrugged. "It was time."

Sandy bent over to the cooler and tossed Ruby a cold beer. "I know, I know, you hate beer, but tonight I think you need one."

Ruby reluctantly popped the top and scanned the area for any signs of Reed. He had not made it yet. She took a big gulp and grimaced. "See, I'm drinking, for crying out loud. Why are you looking at me like that?"

Sandy nudged her shoulder. "So, who are you looking for since you broke up with tall, dark and trouble?"

Ruby whispered into Sandy's ear, "Reed."

Sandy spit out her beer. "Dang, girl, you jump right out of the frying pan into the fire."

"Hardy, har, har, you're so funny." Ruby loved the smell of the bonfire and she looked around, smelling something else. "Someone's burning a joint."

Sandy sat down on the log next to the fire and crossed her ankles, motioning for her to follow suit. "Sit by me. Maybe they'll pass it around. Spill the beans. What happened at Opryland yesterday?"

Ruby told her everything that had happened at Opryland and by the time she had finished, Ruby was on her second beer. She was feeling slightly intoxicated and giddy.

Sandy whistled loudly and several people turned around. "You're going to rip their friendship apart, you know that, right?"

"Sandy, you don't know the whole story," Ruby said. She told Sandy about the game, *Tap It,* and about the first time she met Reed and Brent in the store, about the pool, the first ballgame and the lake. *Tap it* had come to a head yesterday at the park. She also talked about her breakup with Brent and the steamy night with Reed, afterwards.

Sandy's eyes widened. "Holy cow, why didn't you tell me sooner? I could have given you some pointers. I'm not sure if I like them more or less, gutsy sons of bitches, playing women. Almost wished *Tap it* had been my idea." Sandy laughed and threw her arm around Ruby's shoulder. "But it looks like you fell in love with Reed in the process. I'll kill him if he hurts you."

Sandy and Anna opened a couple more beers. Ruby was on the verge of being drunk. She rarely drank and three was always her limit. "You're right, Sandy. I'm in love with Reed. I got it real bad." Ruby's eyelids dropped.

Sandy pulled her closer and then pushed her playfully. "My advice to you is to keep the upper hand, man." Sandy snorted. "Upper hand man. Sounds like the name of a good band."

The music was cranked to a song by Kool and the Gang. Ruby and Sandy began to dance "the bump," and then Ruby began to freestyle. Ruby closed her eyes, grooving to the tunes. As she danced, she felt someone's arm drop around her waist, pressing her bum to his buckle. Ruby turned, expecting to see Reed, and instead found Brent.

Ruby wriggled away from him. "What are you doing here?"

Brent looked at her with a wicked grin. "Ruby Jane, you're drunk."

Ruby straightened her back and squared her shoulders. "I am not. You need to go harass some other girl. Remember, I broke up with you yesterday." She glanced over and saw Reed walking toward them. When Reed saw her talking to Brent, he stopped dead in his tracks.

Brent tried to pull her into his arms and she used her hands to push off his chest. "Stop it, Brent. I mean it. I told you yesterday I didn't want to see you anymore." He held her chin as he bent over, trying to kiss her. She shook her head back and forth.

Jerry walked over to them and said, "Ruby is there a problem?"

Ruby, being a little drunk, said, "Hell yeah, there's a problem. This asshole won't leave me alone."

Jerry's face flushed red as Anna walked up beside him, placing a hand on his arm. She looked over at Ruby. "Honey, what's the matter?"

Brent let his hands drop away as Ruby pointed at him. "He's the matter." But as she turned to walk away from Brent, he grabbed her arm, squeezing it tight. Ruby yelled, "Let go of me!" People began to turn around, and several had moved closer to check out what was going on.

Brent spun her around to him. He jerked her up against him and shouted, "Why don't you shut the hell up!"

Ruby narrowed her eyes at him. "What did you just say to me?" She heard the people chattering around her and felt faintly nauseated. "Brent, please let me go. You're hurting me. I know you're mad at me. Don't be stupid."

Brent noticed Reed and then turned to back Ruby, shouting at her. "Damn it, Ruby, did you meet Reed last night? Did you?" She tried to jerk away from him, but he held on tighter.

Reed stormed over to them and grabbed Brent's shirt. "Let her go. Now."

Brent turned to Reed, still gripping Ruby's arm as she tried to wriggle away.

Reed said, between clenched teeth, "This is the last time I say this, Brent. Let her go."

Brent let Ruby go and pushed her so hard Ruby lost her balance and landed in the grass, very hard on her rump, with an "Oomph" escaping.

Ruby looked up as Reed bent down to check on her. Out of the corner of her eye, she saw Brent's right fist as he landed a punch to Reed's jaw. She screamed, "Stop it! Stop it!"

Reed twisted around swiftly and threw a counter punch to Brent's gut, which landed with a thud, and then Reed tackled him to the ground. They were punching each other when Ruby began to feel violently sick. She rolled onto her hands and knees and puked. Sandy and Anna rushed over to her.

Sandy said to Anna, "Look in one of those coolers and see if you can find her a Coke." She pulled Ruby's hair off her shoulders, as she got sick again. "It's okay, pumpkin. Let it all out."

Ruby felt weak in the knees as she looked over to see George and Jerry pulling Reed and Brent apart. They were staring each other down. She heard her brother tell Brent to leave.

Brent spat on the ground next to Reed's feet. "This ain't over, you son of a bitch."

Reed squared his shoulders. "Anytime you're ready, brother." He turned and ran to Ruby.

RUBY AND REED WALKED SLOWLY over to the creek and sat down. He placed his hand on her thigh. "Are you okay?"

"No, I feel terrible, Reed. I don't want to ruin your friendship with Brent." She looked up at him with sadness.

"Brent should have never touched you. It's his fault. You broke up with him. He hates to lose. He'll either get over or he won't. My only concern right now is you."

Ruby leaned against Reed's shoulder. "I don't drink. I kinda lost my cool. I started it."

Reed stroked her hair, which hung loosely down her back. Then he turned his head toward her and replied in a clipped tone, "There is never a cause for a man to hurt a woman. Ever."

Ruby lay back on the grass and looked up at the stars. They were so close she could almost touch them. She listened to the water as it rushed through the creek, and in the background she heard laughter and "Harvest Moon" by Neil Young being played on someone's car stereo. Reed lay down beside her, staring up at the sky.

Ruby turned on her side toward Reed, placed her hand gently on his cheek, still red from Brent's punch. Her breath hitched. "Thank you for taking up for me tonight." Ruby never thought about the consequences of playing the *Tap It* game. She certainly never intended for Reed and Brent to fight each other over her.

He linked his fingers with hers and then raised her fingers to his lips. "Silly goose, you don't have to thank me. I wanted to kill him for hurting you." With a half laugh he said, "I'm pretty sure he wanted to kill me, too. Thank God, Jerry and your brother pulled us apart. Now, come here and lay your head on my chest. Let me give you some loving."

Ruby laid her head on his chest and she relaxed in his arms while he stroked her hair. She was right where she needed to be.

Chapter 8

Strange Magic

RUBY SPENT THE LAST TWO weeks of summer with Reed. They went swimming, and she took him hiking up to Campbell Ridge. They spent many evenings on the porch at Everglade Farms. Reed had met her parents playing ball with George. She introduced Reed to her grandfather, and Granddaddy seemed to like Reed. Her grandfather told her after one of those visits that Reed seemed to be good people.

By the middle of August, Ruby, Sandy and Anna began moving into their rental house on Bell Street. The house had been built in the 1950s. It was a one-story brick house with hardwood floors and three bedrooms.

Ruby, Sandy and Anna cleaned it thoroughly and applied a fresh coat of paint on the interior walls while their fathers worked on the lawn. They found lawn furniture at a yard sale that worked perfectly on the covered front porch of the house. Anna's daddy had arranged for a man to do the yard work, but it was the girls' responsibility to maintain the interior of the house.

From their three homes, they managed to find enough furniture to fill the rental, including a new color TV Ruby got for her birthday. Ruby's parents bought them a kitchen table and chairs, while the rental company furnished their appliances. They each had their own bedroom, but they had to share the only bathroom.

Moving into the house with her best friends was just what the doctor ordered. Ruby's new classes would be starting soon, and living with her two best friends was going to be so much fun.

After their parents left, the girls rested for about five minutes and then screamed a chorus of "Woo Hoo!"

Anna ran to the portable stereo located in the den. She flipped through their albums and selected Crosby, Stills, Nash and Young and placed the album on the record player. As the music started, Anna threw her hands up in the air and shook her butt. "It is time to crank the jams! We have our own crib!"

They cranked up the music, danced, and then began to cook supper together. Ruby stood at the butcher block table, chopping up tomatoes, mushrooms, and onions, while Anna was at the stove browning the beef and Italian sausage. Sandy had bought the ingredients for margaritas and was making a pitcher for them to drink.

Ruby stopped chopping the vegetables and looked over at her two friends. She reached inside her pocket and brought out her amber stone turning it over in her hand. "Do y'all remember the day we found the room in the cave?" Both Anna and Sandy stopped what they were doing and looked at Ruby and the stone in her hand.

Anna and Sandy both reached inside their pockets, bringing out their own stones. Ruby's eyes widened with alarm as her stone warmed in her hand. "Wow, so, I'm not the only one carrying around the stone we discovered on our spelunking trip to the cave. Don't you think that's strange? My stone warms up when I hold it, does yours?"

Ruby looked down at Anna's amethyst stone. Anna cleared her throat. "Yes, and my amethyst stone glows."

The three girls stood in a circle. Sandy held out her hand to show Anna and Ruby her hiddenite stone. Ruby thought her eyes were playing tricks on her. Sandy's green stone seemed to pulse. Ruby managed to say weakly, "So, I don't think it's a coincidence that we've never mentioned that day in the cave until today. I've tried so many times to talk to y'all, and the words just wouldn't come out." Ruby placed her stone back inside her pocket and went back to the table to chop up the rest of the vegetables. "I started having dreams the night we discovered the hidden room, the totem and the stones. Sometimes my dreams foretell births, sometimes deaths and sometimes I can see the future."

Ruby glanced at Anna and Sandy; both remained silent, and both were wide-eyed with shock. "My life dreams are about the beginning of a life, the creation. Those dreams are so full of light and love, and when I wake up, I have a sense of peace. But my dreams about death, they're dark and full of despair, and I wake in a cold sweat. I have not been able to stop any deaths yet, but I keep trying."

Ruby walked over and dropped the veggies into Anna's frying pan. "I dreamed about Aunt Sammie passing away and the very next day she died. I dreamed about Reed and the next day he walked into the store. I keep having another dream about a man chasing me. I think he wants to kill me. I'm not sure if it's a bad dream or if someone in the future is going to try and kill me. It's freaky."

Anna smiled weakly at Ruby and continued to cook. "The day after the cave, I was sitting on my patio at home and a blue bird dropped out of nowhere onto the concrete. The poor thing had a broken wing. I walked over to it, talking softly, and picked up the bird. The bird wasn't even afraid of me. Then, energy shot to my hands. The energy felt like static electricity but stronger. When the energy finally left and I opened my hands, the bird flew away." Anna shook her head.

Sandy handed a margarita to Anna and then one to Ruby. She grabbed a big pot under the kitchen cabinet for their noodles. Sandy walked over to the kitchen sink and turned on the faucet. After the pot filled with water, she placed it on the back burner of the stove and turned the burner on high. She grabbed her drink and sat at the kitchen table. "It was several days for me before I knew something was different. I was working on a story for the school newspaper. I had to interview one of the teachers, Mr. Kane, for some lame award he was receiving. I think the award was Teacher of the Month. When I finished my interview, I shook his hand. It couldn't have been more than two or three seconds, but I saw flashes of his life. The son of a bitch was a sick pervert. He'd been abusing teenage girls for years. I think he knew or maybe he sensed that I saw what he had done to those girls." Sandy took a big gulp of her drink and then walked to the sink to look out the window.

"I nailed his ass to the cross. I'm not sure how, but I knew exactly where he kept photos of his victims in his house. I typed an anonymous letter, like I was a victim, detailing exactly how he tricked me into his house, what he did to me and the photos he took.

I sent a letter to the local news station, the police department and the school board."

Sandy poured another drink. "He never served a day in prison, because he killed himself."

Anna shook her head. "Jesus preserve us. I wondered how they caught him. The news only mentioned the child abuse and his suicide."

Ruby placed her hand on Sandy's shoulder. "By the pricking of my thumbs, something wicked this way comes."

The girls made the spaghetti but had lost their appetites. Instead, they poured more margaritas and went to sit outside on the covered porch. They lit several candles and two tiki torches.

Ruby sat down on the white wicker loveseat and kicked her legs out in front of her. "Wonder why we were chosen. Why do we have these abilities and why weren't we able to talk about them until now? The carved figure from the cave appears in my dreams. He's not a god, but some kind of messenger, revealing both good and evil. In my life dreams, he makes me feel hopeful, and when I see the future, those dreams are so vivid and detailed, it's like I've been given a choice to leave the future to fate or intervene. I'm still trying to wrap my head around the death dreams."

Anna took a deep breath and leaned forward, placing her hands on her thighs. "I've had one other episode, and it involved my mom. We were cleaning up supper dishes and Mom dropped a Pyrex dish. It broke on the floor. She reached down to pick up the shards of glass and one slipped out of her hand and cut a gash in her arm. She screamed for Dad, but I rushed over to her, wrapping my hands around the cut, blood pouring through my fingertips. The energy surging into my hands made our lights go out, but I didn't let go of her until I felt the power leave me. When the lights finally came on, the gash was completely gone. My mother passed out. I scared my parents. Whatever this power is, we never spoke about it again. It was as if that whole scene never happened."

Sandy grabbed the pitcher of margaritas off the table and topped off their drinks again. She took another sip and said, "Well, on the flip side, I have had good readings, too. I see things when I hold someone's hands."

Sandy sat down between Ruby and Anna, placing her glass on the wicker coffee table. "We need to start a diary of everything we have experienced since the cave and log in every time something new happens. We may be able to see some kind of pattern, some kind of link of how this is supposed to work. We may be able to figure a way to link our gifts. I will buy a journal this week." Sandy laughed. "We'll call it the *Ditch Lane Diaries*." Ruby and Anna both laughed at the name.

Ruby said, "I agree. We need to write down everything. The last frightening dream I had was at the lake this summer. There were violent storms, booming thunder and crashes of lightning. I could hear people wailing. The dream terrified me. Thankfully, it hasn't come true. I'm kinda paranoid about dreaming now. I'm just glad we can finally talk to each other."

Anna replied quickly, "My power doesn't always work. But I do feel my power getting stronger every time I use it." They both looked at Sandy.

Sandy said, "The pervert was the worst. I've had a couple of random readings, but nothing alarming."

Ruby thought for a moment, and said, "So, I'm the dreamer, Anna's the healer and Sandy's the soul reader. Thank God, we don't live in the 1600s or we'd be burned at the stake."

Sandy raised her glass and stood up. "To the *Ditch Lane Diaries*. May we grow in knowledge and use our powers to help others. And to figure out what the heck this messenger wants from us."

Ruby and Anna stood to join her and said in chorus, "To the *Ditch Lane Diaries*."

Chapter 9

Tonight's The Night

MTSU WAS LOCATED IN THE heart of Tennessee and was home to the Blue Raiders. When the fall semester classes started, Ruby's life quickly became hectic. She managed to juggle her household chores and class workload relatively smoothly. Ruby, Anna and Sandy had been together for so long the transition to them living together went very well.

Ruby had a full load of classes on Mondays, Wednesdays, and Fridays, with her labs falling on Tuesdays and Thursdays. Ruby and Reed walked to class together, and they met for lunch in the campus grill or on the grounds nearly every day. They studied together in the Todd Library, and on the weekends they would go to parties or to area nightclubs with Anna, Jerry and Sandy. Ruby had never been so happy in her life.

One afternoon, she sat under a big maple in The Grove next to Peck Hall, waiting for Reed to get out of class. The Grove was a favorite place for students to study, eat lunch or just hang out together. The autumn air was still warm and streaks of light from the sun shone through the huge shade trees. Ruby was leaning against a big tree trunk reading a book, when Brent came up beside her and joined her on the ground.

"Whatcha reading, sweet girl?' Brent wore an off-white, V-neck sweater, with the sleeves pushed up to his elbows, Levi's, and cowboy boots. His tan against the sweater set off his jet-black hair, which was blowing gently in the wind. She angled her chin to meet Brent's gaze at eye level.

Ruby dog-eared her place in the book. "*Dorian Gray*, English Lit. How are you?" She didn't want to be mad at him anymore.

Brent pulled at the stems from the freshly mown grass and glanced back up to her eyes. "I'm so sorry about the party, Ruby. I shouldn't have talked to you so crudely or grabbed your arm. I was jealous and pissed off. Forgive me?"

Ruby smoothed her ponytail, twirling the ends with her fingers. "I forgive you. Do you forgive me? I didn't mean to cause problems between you and Reed."

Several female students walked by them and one said, "Hi, Brent." Ruby smiled in spite of herself. The boy *was* darn good-looking. Girls couldn't help themselves.

Brent threw the girls a peace sign and turned back to Ruby. He asked, "So, are you still in love? Reed treating you okay?"

Ruby looked down at the grass for a second. She hated to see the disappointment in his eyes and knew she'd been the one who had put it there. "Yeah, still in love. He's been great, so far. You seeing anyone?"

With a sigh, he replied, "I see several girls, but none of them are you. I miss you, RJ. I miss you so much. I didn't realize how much I enjoyed just being with you, laughing with you and just goofing off. Most of the girls I date, they don't give a shit about me as a person. They just like the way I look. That never mattered to you."

She had to chuckle. "Oh, Brent, I like the way you look, too. You'll find the person you're supposed to be with. I know it." She placed her hand on his forearm, and he covered it with his hand. Her hand dropped away.

Brent gave her a serious glance. "I wanted to spend my life with you. I don't want you to feel sorry for me. It's just hard knowing you're with him. Do you ever think about me? Do you miss me? I'm not even mad at him. Hell, I don't blame him. After three years of *Tap It*, it took a fiery redhead to blow us both out of the water. And speak of the devil; he's walking pretty fast in this direction now." Brent laughed as Ruby's mouth curved into a smile.

Ruby could hear a steady stream of curses coming from Reed's mouth. She stood up and hadn't missed the speculative glance Reed had thrown her way. Ruby reached out to touch his arm. "Reed, Brent just stopped by to apologize."

Reed gave her a thin smile and then turned to Brent. "So, you're sorry for putting a bruise on her arm. Did you know you hurt her?"

Brent squared his shoulders, and Ruby knew she had to do something quickly. "Reed, he is sorry. It's okay. You two have been friends a long time. Now, kiss and make up." She placed her hands on her hips, which made them both laugh.

Brent took a step back. "No thanks, *Mom*, I'm not kissing him. I'll leave you two alone." He turned and walked away.

Ruby sat back down on the grass and Reed sat beside her. He was breathing hard. Strands of her hair escaped her ponytail from the wind. She smoothed them down with her hand. She moistened her lips, but her mouth was still dry from the darkened look Reed gave her. "Reed, don't be mad at me. I was sitting here reading when he sat down beside me. He was only here a few minutes before you arrived."

Reed lifted a brow and said in a clipped tone, "I don't trust the son of a bitch. He would try to steal you from me in a New York minute."

Ruby reached up and combed her fingers through his hair and his darkened mood began to soften. She pushed him back on the grass and straddled him. She bent over close to his face and said, "I love you, not him." She kissed him in front of anyone who wanted to look on.

THE WEEK BEFORE HOMECOMING, RUBY took Reed hiking around her favorite trails. They walked along the river trail for about a half hour until they found the perfect place to stretch out. Ruby brought a stadium blanket in her backpack, and Reed had filled his backpack with drinks and snacks. They lay under the trees next to the water and relaxed in each other's arms.

Reed drew her closer to him and said, "I've lived here for three years and I've never seen this trail. It's so beautiful."

Ruby sat up and pulled a bottle of water out of her backpack. She gulped it down. "It is beautiful out here. I love to hike. I've walked most of the trails around this county and a few off-trails too. I love the woodsy smells of the trees and wildflowers." Reed handed her an apple and she took a bite. The crisp apple burst with sweetness inside her mouth. She took another bite as she surveyed the area around them.

Ruby pointed to a couple of nearby plants that were native to the area. "This beauty here is the Tennessee coneflower, and look over here, see that gem? It's the little bluestem, and oh, oh, look over there in the river! Do you see the little otter?"

Reed chuckled as he tore into his candy bar. "He's a cute little fella, isn't he? And you amaze me. How do you know the names of all those plants?" He took another bite of his candy bar and rummaged in his backpack to pull out a bottle of orange juice.

With a shrug, she said, "I took horticulture in high school and kinda got addicted to researching the flowers and plants native to the area. It's one of my hobbies. I've helped my mom over the years experiment with transplanting some of the wildflowers and grasses in her yard. I love being outside, planting flowers and digging in the dirt."

Reed lay back on the blanket, placing his hand behind his head and looking up into the blue sky. "I love you."

She whipped her head around to face him. "You've never said that to me before. Do you really love me?" A gust of wind kicked up some leaves and a squirrel darted out and scurried up a nearby tree.

With a lazy smile, he said, "I have loved you since the moment I saw you in the store. It just took me a while to admit it to myself."

She lay back next to him, looking out at nature. This had turned into a perfect autumn day and she would never forget it. Reed loved her.

RUBY AND REED TOOK TURNS visiting each other over the next several weeks, either at her place or his apartment. They had had some pretty hot and heavy make-out sessions, but she had yet to sleep with him.

Then Reed invited her to spend the weekend with him in Nashville. He bought tickets for them to see Bob Seger and had booked a room at the Hyatt Regency. He'd also booked a reservation to the spinning restaurant above the hotel, which offered a spectacular view of the Nashville skyline. Ruby decided this would be the weekend she would make love to him.

As that Friday night approached, Ruby became nervous and just a little frightened. She had already talked to Sandy, who had somewhat prepared her for what would happen. She had taken anatomy, but the clinical version of sex was different when you were the one it was going to happen to.

Ruby typically wore blue jeans when she and Reed were together. Friday night was going to be special. She wanted to look and feel special. Ruby had received, for her birthday, a beautiful long, off-white maxi which had buttons down the entire length of the dress. She paired it with a brown leather belt and her dark brown cowboy boots. Sandy and Anna had done her hair and makeup.

Her two friends brought her to the full-length mirror behind Sandy's bedroom door. Anna placed her hand on Ruby's shoulder. "You are stunning tonight."

Sandy hugged her. "Our baby is leaving here a girl and will be returning to us a woman."

"Geez Louise. Come on y'all, I'm nervous enough." Ruby turned around and playfully pushed Sandy out of the way to look at her reflection in the mirror.

Sandy and Anna followed her out on the front porch as Reed pulled into the driveway. Sandy teased, "Poor Reed doesn't have a clue, does he?"

Bags in hand, Ruby said, "Well, I'm pretty sure he knows I'm going to sleep with him this weekend. I just didn't tell him the part about being a virgin."

"God, I'd love to see the expression on his face when he finally realizes he has a virgin on his hands." Sandy cackled and Ruby gave Sandy a mock elbow to the ribs.

"Check ya later, much later!" Ruby sucked in her breath when she saw Reed. His hair was shiny as silk, and his expression was bright with excitement. Reed wore a tan corduroy jacket with a black turtleneck, paired with Levi's and penny loafers. Tonight's the night, she thought.

"You ready to go, Ruby?" Reed jogged up her front steps, and then he froze in his tracks. "Oh God, you're a knockout in that dress." She could see the raw hunger in his eyes and giggled when he had to adjust his package. "Let me grab your bags. Huh, um, crap, you've made me lose my train of thought, woman." Ruby blushed, turned to her friends and winked. Reed rushed around to the passenger side of his car and opened the door for her. As she stepped into the car, he placed her bags in the trunk. Ruby waved to Sandy and Anna. Reed jumped into the car, started the engine and pulled out on Bell Street.

AS THEY WALKED INTO THE lobby to check in, Ruby and Reed both raised their heads to watch the glass elevators scale the hotel's twenty-eight floors. Reed held her hand as they walked to the counter. They had just enough time to check into their room and meet their six thirty reservation, with five minutes to spare. The concert started at eight and they were within walking distance.

The spinning restaurant offered them a panoramic view of Nashville and they didn't even have to leave their seats. Reed ordered them a couple of glasses of champagne. Ruby ordered freshwater trout and rice pilaf, with coconut cream pie for dessert. Reed opted for the filet mignon with asparagus spears, roast potatoes and a decadent-looking chocolate cake.

Ruby placed her hand over her stomach. "The food was so delicious. I love it up here. I'm kinda glad we're walking to the concert to burn off some of this pie. How much time do we have?"

Reed waved to the waiter and asked for the bill. "Not much. We should be able to get there in about fifteen minutes. I'm not sure if Seger has a warm-up band. I'm so glad you liked dinner. My parents and I came up here last spring." Reed placed the money in the server folder with the bill. "Come on, let's go, pretty girl."

Bob Seger rocked the house. Sometimes they danced in their seats, and the other times they stood up and looked on, screaming along with the other fans. She and Reed always had such a good time together. He made her laugh all the time. Laughter should never be underestimated.

After the concert, they walked back to their hotel hand-in-hand. The Nashville streets were still full of people. Several musicians were playing acoustic guitars at the corner near their hotel. Reed and Ruby listened as they strummed a George Jones song. After the song ended, Reed put money in their guitar case and placed his hand on the small of Ruby's back, ushering her into the hotel lobby.

Reed guided her to the hotel lounge. "Let's get a nightcap before we head back upstairs." He ordered them brandy.

Reed seemed as nervous as she was. Ruby took the glass from him and she quickly drank the shot.

He laughed. "Ruby, I want you relaxed, not passed out."

Ruby felt the sweet, warm rush of alcohol seep into her bloodstream in an instant. "Well, I'm relaxed. I promise not to pass out." She leaned across the bar and ordered a glass of water. The lounge had deep mahogany walls and the recessed lighting had been set low. The candles on each table were lit in beautiful crystal hurricanes which cast a soft glow across the room. A man played a sweet, soft melody on the piano.

Reed brushed his lips against her cheek. "Would you like to dance?"

Ruby glanced around and didn't see anyone else dancing. "Reed, I'm not sure we're supposed to dance in here."

He swooped his arm around her waist, and the next minute they were dancing on the small floor. The piano player smiled at Reed and nodded. Reed held her hand curled next to his face and his other hand rested low, right above her behind. They swayed slowly back and forth to the sad, sweet tune.

Reed buried his face in her hair. "You're so beautiful. I'm the luckiest man on earth right now, with you in my arms."

She was enjoying herself. "You're going to get lucky," she teased. Ruby placed her hands on his hips and linked her fingers in his pant loops, pulling him closer to her.

"Mmmm, I love the sound of that. Feeling a little frisky, are ya?"

Ruby rose on tiptoe, placed her lips close to his ear, and said, "Very frisky." Reed bent over and kissed her.

After paying their bar tab, they walked in silence to the elevators. Once inside, they were alone as they watched the floors zoom past them. He whispered in her ear, "Tell me, Ruby...tell me you want me to make love to you tonight."

She turned to face him and her arms went up around his neck. "I want you to make love to me, more than anything else in this whole wide world, Reed Jackson. I want to feel you inside of me."

They ran from the elevators to their hotel room. The room was dark, except for the Nashville skylights. Reed walked over and flipped on the little light on the table beside the bed. He turned, and the look he gave her had the air backing up in her lungs.

"Reed, I'll only be a minute." Ruby closed the bathroom door and looked at her reflection in the mirror. Her cheeks flushed, and her skin heated. Ruby had left her night bag in the bathroom before they went to dinner, so she pulled out the new, luscious, ivory silk and lace chemise she had bought for tonight.

The body-kissing A-line skimmed her thighs and felt amazing next to her skin. She hoped Reed loved it. Her see-through lace panties stretched perfectly over her curves. She thought it was perfectly cheeky and giggled. She brushed her teeth and hair and took a deep breath and she walked back into the bedroom. Reed stood shirtless closing the blinds, and then he turned around sucking in a deep breath.

Reed's eyes wandered over her, as she stood across the room. She could barely breathe, and she couldn't wait to touch him. Reed had a body that would make Adonis weep with jealousy. She grinned smugly at him and pressed her hand against the wall. "So, I gather you like what you see?"

"Honey, you are truly beautiful. I have no words sufficient enough to express how truly beautiful you are to me. And you're so incredibly sexy in that lingerie, I think I could probably rip it off with my teeth pretty damn quick." He crossed the room to her in two strides and pulled her up tight against him. He inhaled deeply and then slid his hands around her bottom, giving her a gentle squeeze. "Kiss me, Ruby."

Reed ran his fingers through her hair to the nape of her neck. He slanted his mouth over hers and slid his warm tongue deep into her mouth with slow strokes and she met him with demanding strokes of her own. Her hunger for him grew wilder with every passing second. She was fiercely clutching his arms; even with their bodies melted to one another she wanted to be closer, pulling at him. She could feel her heartbeat hammer so loudly in her ears. His thigh muscle tensed against her until he trembled. She pushed him slightly away so she could view him. His skin felt hot under her touch as her fingers traced over his powerful chest.

"Reed, you're so gorgeous." He unzipped his pants, his rock-hard erection responding to her compliment as they fell away to the floor. This was the first time Ruby had seen a man, up close and personal. She ran her hands over his thighs and his glutes tightened. She followed her urge to touch him and reached out, placing her hand around him. He let out a moan. She never had a man of her very own and she ran her hand over him. His skin felt velvety smooth and Reed stilled her hand.

His voice was low and husky. "Not fair, princess. You've seen mine. Now it's my turn to see yours."

They stood facing each other as he slowly began to slide her chemise off her shoulders. It fell to the floor. His lips slid down her neck to the tender place in her throat and then back up to her mouth. She wanted to close her eyes to his touch but was too curious and anxious she'd miss something. She stood before Reed, tall and proud.

Reed ran his finger over her breast. "Do you want me as bad as I want you?" The look in his eyes drove every thought from her brain.

His ravenous perusal of her body made her stomach muscles clench tight. He began to gently caress her breasts, and then he leaned over and placed her breast in his mouth. She closed her eyes and arched her back as he suckled her nipple. Her skin felt like it was being turned inside out as she shivered with pleasure. Reed caressed her with his expert tongue and then moved his mouth to her other breast. Ruby became molten liquid under his touch and took a deep breath, she smelled him—soap, Aramis, and man.

Ruby sighed. "Mmm, that feels so good." Reed chuckled against her skin. "Oh, Reed." Her fingers twisted in his hair and her response was met with him devouring her breasts. Something deep inside her throbbed and shivers shot up her spine.

He was driving her crazy with desire, and then he dropped to the floor on his knees and slowly removed her panties with his teeth. "Oh, you're so wet. You're killing me."

Her knees buckled when his fingers slipped over her outer folds. She looked down at him. "Killing you? Geesh, I can barely stand up."

Reed stood and scooped her up in his arms and laid her gently on the bed. She felt weightless as he began to press feather-light kisses along her inner thighs. Ever so slowly, he trailed his fingers over her legs and then under her knees toward her bottom. He pressed her legs open wider, and then he trailed his tongue along the most intimate part of her.

She was so restless under his touch and his hands seemed to be everywhere, which drove her insane. He pressed kisses against her, tasting her. She cried out, gripping and twisting the sheets in her fists as he stroked her. She had uncontrollable passion for him. She felt wildness in her. It was wonderful and terrifying—demanding, but still so tender.

She wiggled under him when she heard him make a "yummy" sound and had to bite her tongue not to laugh. The most insane thoughts ran through her mind. She felt intense love and desire, and at the same time, embarrassment and laughter—all of these new emotions rolled up in one.

Ruby had a "Reed fever"—when she heard him say, "Mmmm," his voice vibrating against her skin. He was kissing her with his delicious mouth between her legs, making her moan and arch against him. Ruby's muscles were tightening and contracting. Something was building inside of her, higher and higher, until she felt an explosion of vibrations. Then the freaking dam broke and she shuddered against him as wave after wave of pleasure rushed from her. Reed's fingers slid over her soft flesh with artful strokes and her insides throbbed and pulsed against him. Her skin was so taut, threatening to split her apart.

Reed lifted her bottom off the bed and her muscles began to quiver, violently. He held onto her for another moment until she could take it no longer. She grabbed onto his hair and screamed out his name. Her mind had escaped into a dream world feeling the aftershocks of her orgasm rock her, leaving her weak in sated bliss.

"You're the sweetest, honey. Did you like that love?" He rose above her, crawling his way up the bed to position himself over her.

"Uh huh." She finally opened her eyes to see he had risen above her. His bulging biceps were placed on either side of her shoulders.

REED NUZZLED AGAINST HER NECK, taking little nips, and then he moved his mouth to her ear, running his tongue on the inside. She was the most beautiful woman he had ever seen. It had taken all of his control not to just plunge hard and deep inside of her. He had never wanted to make love to someone so bad in his life. He whispered, "I love you, Ruby Jane." He positioned himself, slowly sinking inside her—and then met the resistance of her hymen.

Reed's eyes flew wide open and he jerked back. "You're a virgin?" he said, in shock, trying to scramble away from her.

Ruby held onto him tightly as he was trying to quickly extract himself from her grip. "Stay inside me, please. I've dreamed of this moment with you, and that's not a line. It's the truth. I had a dream about you the night before I met you at the general store. Reed, you're my destiny." She looked up at him with a shy expression and her cheeks flushed pink and her look hit him hard between his ribs.

Reed stilled and his eyes softened; his voice was barely a whisper. "Ruby, darling, are you sure?"

Ruby nodded her head yes and ran her hands down his arms. "I want you. That is all I'm sure of."

Reed pushed deep inside her and broke the barrier between them. He sank deeper and Ruby cried out. He stilled, again, his heart filled with so much emotion.

"I'm so sorry, honey." His eyes watered as he gazed down at her. "I don't want to hurt you, ever."

"Please don't apologize. I couldn't stay a virgin forever."

A tear spilled over her cheek and he stopped it with his lips. "You're my girl, you hear me? You're mine." Reed bent over, gently brushing his lips across her cheek and back to her mouth as he languorously slid inside her. He murmured in her ear that it would be okay. He told her how much he loved her and he would always take care of her.

He had seen her fear, but she gave way to such tenderness and love that mirrored in his own eyes. Ruby began to move underneath him, following his rhythm as he rocked his hips slowly back and forth.

Reed clamped his arm around her, bringing her closer to him. "I'm not sure I can hold on much longer." He kissed her deeply, pulling her lower lip with his teeth. He held her hips, stretching his fingers across her bottom. She felt so good and he wanted to go wild, but didn't. Being inside of her so tight and warm sent him out of his mind with desire. He kissed her neck, and then he slowly ran his tongue across her lips and inside her mouth.

Ruby couldn't tear her eyes away from him his gaze. Her eyes were bright and her pupils were huge and glazed over with desire. Making love to her was more than he could have ever imagined. His movements were painstakingly slow. With a half cry, she said, "Reed, I love you so much."

Reed had been holding himself in check, pacing himself as he eased in and out of her. Her long slender fingers were digging into his back as his movements became faster until at last, with one hard thrust, his body tightened and he cried out her name. His muscles relaxed and Reed collapsed on top of her. He rolled onto his back and pulled her under his arm. She rested her head on his chest, and he said, "Geez Louise."

A SMILE CURVED RUBY LIPS. Reed had just uttered Ruby's favorite two words. They lay in each other's arms. He adjusted the angle of his face to look more clearly in her eyes.

With a look of concern, he said, "Next time, honey, I promise you'll feel nothing but pleasure. If I had known, Ruby—you didn't tell me. Why?"

She took a deep breath and replied, "I didn't want to scare you away. Would you have slept with me if you had known I was a virgin?"

He teased, "Probably not. I would have run for the hills."

Reed stroked her hair, and right before she drifted off to sleep, she heard him say in a whisper, "I love you, Ruby Jane."

RUBY STRETCHED HER ARMS OUT and rolled over in the bed. She felt wonderful. Like all was right with the world. She glanced over at the clock on the nightstand and it read eight o'clock. She didn't want to sleep the entire weekend away.

Reed rolled over and pulled her next to his chest and nudged his face against her cheek. "I'm going to draw us a hot bath. The warm water will help to ease any soreness and, well, I can't wait to get you naked in the bathtub!"

She laughed, and said, "Oo-kay, that sounds lovely and a little wicked." She grabbed for her lingerie, but he stopped her.

"You won't need any clothes, darling. I want to see you." He pushed the covers off the bed and traced the line of her curves. "Baby, you're too sweet. I'm not going to be able to keep my hands off of you." His voice made her insides quiver.

She pushed him back on the bed. "My turn." She noticed instantly her perusal had aroused him.

"Are you through ogling me, woman? Let's get in the bathtub." He shot her a grin and got out of bed.

Reed started running the water into the bathtub. He sat on the edge and poured in some bubble bath from the hotel.

Ruby watched him, in all his glory. "Bubble bath, eh?"

With a lifted eyebrow, he said, "Yeah, I thought we might as well take full advantage of our stay here."

Ruby massaged the muscles in his neck and he rolled his head back. "That feels so good." He motioned her to the tub. "After you, princess."

Ruby kissed his head and stepped into the tub. She slid down until the water covered everything, except her head. "This is completely divine. Come in with me."

"I'm coming. I just want to get a few towels." Reed grabbed them a couple of towels, rolled one up, and stepped into the tub behind her. He scooted her back between his legs, sliding down a little to let the water run over both of their bodies. Ruby relaxed against his chest and he caressed her.

Reed ran his hands up and down her arms, lathering up her skin with the scented soap. "How are you feeling this morning? Do you hurt very badly?"

Ruby placed her hands over his. "No, not really. I feel fine. The water does make me feel good, and I love having you next to me. I'm better than all right. I'm great!"

The hotel bathroom was lit with recessed lights, and there was a full-length mirror along one wall. A warm tan tile covered the other walls and the floor was marble. Ruby felt like a princess in the beautiful hotel room.

Ruby flipped over, sliding around on his chest to face him. Reed made the "yummy" sound again and she giggled. "Reed, you've made that sound three times."

"It's because you're so freaking delicious." He ran his hands down her back, scooping her butt cheeks in his hands and sliding her up to him for a kiss.

"I thought after we checked out today, we could go walk Broadway, have a drink at Tootsie's and walk along the riverfront. What do you say?" Reed asked.

Ruby said teasingly, "Mmm, sounds delicious." A smile touched her lips. "Do you think we could try making love again before we leave?"

"Ruby, I've never slept with a virgin before. I didn't want to—I don't want to hurt you." He gently embraced her.

"I'm not a china doll. I won't break." Ruby moved atop him. She brushed her lips over his and she could see the darkening of his eyes. She wanted to give herself to him, not just the making love part, which was killer. But when they were joined together, it felt as though they became one person, one soul.

Reed was so gentle with her. He scooped her out of the tub and carefully dried her off. Reed picked up her hairbrush and began to brush out her hair. He placed scented lotion on his hands and began to apply it to her shoulders and then her back. He poured more lotion on his hands and moved to her chest, caressing her breasts as she lolled her head back. He rubbed lotion over her stomach and then down to the V where her thighs joined.

Ruby closed her eyes to the wonderful pleasure it gave her, having his hands on her. He held her foot in his hand, massaging the lotion into her heel, and then applied more lotion to his hands, rubbing her calf muscles and then her thighs. He pulled her to a standing position and rubbed her bum with the remaining lotion on his hands.

Reed carried her into the bedroom, laid her down on the bed and stretched out beside her. His kiss was as soft as a whisper. His hands gingerly caressed her arms as he ran his fingers up to her shoulders. Then he massaged her neck for a moment before he continued to her back. His hands moved lightly down her thighs, making her moan in vexation.

Reed moved with the grace of a dancer, tracing her lips with his tongue, nibbling on her bottom and then her top lip. She ran her hand over his biceps and down his back in a pitiful attempt to mimic his moves.

Ruby had a flicker of a premonition while he made love to her. Ruby knew in her heart that she would marry this man. She wanted to spend the rest of her life with Reed. Images flashed in her mind of her having his children, and growing old with him, and she wasn't even holding the amber stone. She had found her home.

REED WATCHED RUBY'S FACE AS he slowly seduced her. He wanted to please her. He wanted her to enjoy every caress, every touch of his fingers and his mouth. Every inch of her was the sweetest nectar to his lips. When his finger slipped inside her, a cry ripped out of her. He watched as she writhed and Reed fed on her pleasure. He was flying, soaring high above the clouds with emotion. He had never experienced such an amazing feeling before with anyone else, only with her as he locked onto her beautiful brown eyes.

Ruby was his now, and his alone. He had only known her for a few months, but he was in love with her. He loved her more than his own life. He would kill for her and would gladly die for her. He didn't verbalize these feelings but allowed the love from his fingers, his lips and mouth to speak the words for him.

Reed enjoyed the look of pure satisfaction that lit Ruby's face; it was the most erotic moment of his life when she broke apart, feeling her reach ecstasy. He couldn't wait any longer; he needed to be inside her. Reed pressed himself against her silkiness and sunk deep inside her, claiming her so completely. Ruby loved him, and her love made him the happiest man alive. She filled the air he breathed, consuming him. He had been unable to resist her. He had been unable to stay away from her. Being with Ruby just felt right as he went over the edge of desire.

THE SUNDAY NIGHT AFTER RETURNING home from their excursion to

Nashville, Ruby and Reed decided to go out and eat Italian food. They walked into Tony's Restaurant and Reed asked the waitress to seat them in her darkest corner and then squeezed Ruby's derriere. Since it was after rush hour, the restaurant had their jukebox fired up. The restaurant had white-and-red-checkered tablecloths and candles were lit in dark red glass globes. There were only a couple of tables occupied.

The waitress looked dreamily at Reed and placed them at the largest table in the restaurant. To the waitress's credit, it was dark. They ordered a large pizza, a pitcher of beer and a large Coke for Ruby.

Ruby was sitting so close to Reed, she was practically in his lap. When the pizza came out, he was nibbling Ruby's neck. The waitress's eyes flashed wide at Reed and then at Ruby. She quickly placed the food on the table and then disappeared back into the kitchen.

Reed murmured in Ruby's ear, "You're just too sweet, woman. You're addictive. I want you right now." He ran his hand up from her thigh to the V where her legs met. She stopped him from moving farther into dangerous territory.

His words made her melt against his shoulder. Ruby looked around and said, "Behave yourself. We're in public, for crying out loud."

She squirmed a little before grabbing a slice and taking a bite of pizza. "Pizza is my favorite food and this is sooo good." She woofed down the first slice and reached for another.

Reed grabbed a slice from the pizza pan and took a bite. He closed his eyes for a moment and then he grabbed the pitcher of beer and poured another mug. He laughed. "You eat more than any woman I know."

Ruby looked at him out of the corner of her eye, with cheese hanging off the side of her mouth. "Most women eat. They're just too bashful to eat in front of guys. I don't have a bashful bone in my body."

Reed circled an arm around her shoulder and then leaned in and licked the cheese off her mouth. "Yeah, I kinda noticed."

When the waitress cleared the table, Reed poured one more beer and then placed his hand on Ruby's thigh, rubbing back and forth.

She loved the warm feeling she got when he affectionately touched her. Reed had started nibbling on her ear again, when she giggled and looked up to see Brent staring down at her.

Brent stood with his hands shoved in his pockets. He was with two girls and a guy she had never met. "Having fun?"

Reed leaned back against the booth and pulled Ruby under his arm. With a laugh, he said, "Yeah, we're having a blast."

"Then you won't mind if we join you." Brent directed his next comment to Reed. "I mean, what's a little fight between friends, really." Brent sat down across from them and the other people followed him. "Reed, this is Patti and Rachel, and you remember Brad."

Reed pulled his hand away from Ruby's shoulder. "Brad, this is Ruby. Brad's the one who introduced me to Brent when we were freshmen."

Patti's eyes widened and then she said, "Hold the phone, you're Reed Jackson? Oh, every girl on campus has heard of you because of Tammy Wright. She's told our entire sorority about you." Patti's eyes dropped down toward Reed's lap and then back up to Reed's eyes. She smiled and said, "So, glad to finally meet you." She reached her hand out to shake Reed's, and then she looked at Ruby. "Lucky girl."

Ruby straightened in her seat and quickly put her arm around Reed's shoulder, playing with his hair. "Ain't I, though." Ruby flashed Patti a brilliant smile and inched just a little closer to Reed. He laughed and reached over and kissed Ruby.

Brent looked annoyed at Patti. "What's this, the Reed Jackson adoration society? God, man, what do you do to these women?" Brent stared at Ruby, studying her face.

Reed ignored Brent and turned to Brad. "Still in the dorm?"

Brad looked from Reed to Brent, and said, "Yeah. My parents aren't going to pay for a place for me to live. I'll be living there until I graduate. At least this year, I'm the RA, with my own unit and bathroom. How's Steve?"

Reed held Ruby's hand under the table, running his thumb back and forth against her skin. "He went home this weekend. His dad called because one of their mares is in foal. He wanted to be there when the colt was born."

Ruby noticed Brent's anger and knew he was getting ready to

explode. Brent said maliciously, "So, you have the place all to yourself. How convenient for y'all."

Reed's gaze flickered to Ruby and then back to Brent. "We stayed in Nashville this weekend. We went to a Bob Seger concert and had dinner at the Tower." Ruby wished Reed would keep his mouth shut. Reed reminded her of an alpha wolf staking his claim.

Brent's jaw muscle ticked, and then he said through gritted teeth, "Wow, very impressive, even for you, Reed." He turned his daggers to Ruby. "I knew something looked different about you, honey. So, I guess you're finally celebrating becoming a woman."

Ruby's temper flared. She jumped up and threw her Coke in Brent's face. Patti and Rachel's mouths dropped open. Ruby raised her voice. "You're such an asshole!" She stormed out the door.

REED LEANED OVER TO BRENT before he left the table. "I'll kill you if you ever talk to her like that again."

Brent wiped the Coke off his face with napkins. "Anytime you think you're man enough, bring it on."

Reed ran out of the restaurant and found Ruby leaning against his car. "Don't worry about him; it's a wasted effort. I'm sorry. I should have kept my mouth shut. My vanity got the best of me. Forgive me?"

"There's nothing to forgive. Brent is never going to stop being mad at me. I hurt him. But right now, the only thing hurting him is his pride. Wonder what Patti and Rachel thought."

Reed frowned at her and crossed his arms. His eyes flashed with anger. "That matters because…?"

"It doesn't matter. I was just curious." Ruby shoulder-bumped him. "You jealous?"

"Hell, yes. Get in the car, damn it." Reed had never been mad at her before. He had never had this overpowering feeling of jealousy in his life. Ruby was his woman. She placed her hand out to stop him.

"Reed, I was just kidding." She reached over and kissed him.

His expression softened and he relaxed. He trailed the outline of her jaw with his finger. "Sorry, I get a little mad thinking about you and him this past summer. I know he won't stop either. He still thinks this is a game. I know him. He is going to try and get you back. I could kill him, just thinking about it."

Reed's hand was trembling. Ruby covered his hand with hers and gave him a squeeze. "This isn't a game, remember?"

As Reed walked around to get inside the car, he glanced up and saw Brent staring at Ruby through the glass door of Tony's restaurant. A slow smile lit Brent's face.

Chapter 10

Boogie Nights

RUMORS HAD BEEN FLOATING AROUND about Reed cheating on her from the day they became an item. Ruby knew it was probably Brent or Tammy behind most of the gossip. Reed had spent most of his free time with Ruby, so she didn't know when he would have had the time or the energy to cheat. But he had acted suspiciously when she walked up on him talking to Tammy in the campus bookstore. Ruby had pushed those thoughts out of her mind, because she loved him. He had told her he was in love with her and that she was his girl.

Ruby had developed a voracious appetite for Reed. They were constantly touching each other or kissing. Sandy would get so worked up about their blatant display of affection that when Ruby and Reed would walk into the Bell Street house, Sandy would start humming the theme to *Love Story*.

Ruby and Reed had been dating for two months when he received a call, the Thursday before fall break. "Honey, I have to go home. Mom's been rushed to the hospital."

With a look of concern, she said, "Oh God, what happened?"

"Dad said she is having gallbladder surgery." He ran his fingers through his hair and his brows furrowed with worry.

Her voice trembled. "Please let me go with you."

"No, honey, I don't know how long I'll be gone. I need you to go to school and get my class assignments from my professors. I also need you to go to the marketing department and tell Sarah. She will cover for me at work." He hugged her tightly and she looked up to see tears in his eyes.

"Reed, she is going to be fine. I will start praying, too." She also thought, if needed, she would drive Anna to Knoxville. Anna could use her healing abilities to save her. Ruby's heart was breaking for him.

Once Reed arrived in Knoxville he called Ruby. His mother was in recovery and she would be going home in a couple of days. Ruby was thankful his mother had made it through her surgery. She had seen the strain in Reed's eyes before he left her. Reed loved his mother and respected her. It made Ruby love him more.

While Reed was out of town, Sandy and Anna decided to take her to a new nightclub. The girls had not been out together in months. Jerry had finally gotten enough nerve to ask Anna out, so she had spent her free time dating him. Sandy had become the editor in chief of the school newspaper. She was constantly working to meet deadlines and breaking news stories.

Ruby preferred Levi's and a long-sleeved flannel on a Friday night, but getting dolled up and going dancing with her buddies would be good for her. Sandy and Anna beat Ruby getting dressed. Sandy had on a silky black jumpsuit with a wide black leather belt and wide silver hoop earrings. Anna wore a winter white halter top dress with a gold belt and gold hoop earrings. Since they were both dressed, they turned their attention to Ruby.

The girls picked out one of Sandy's dresses for Ruby, a long red silky dress with slits to the thigh on both sides. The dress had been designed to flare out when the wearer twirled. They paired it with a wide black belt, silver hoop earrings, and black sling-back heels.

Sandy fired up the stereo to play a song by Donna Summer, and she proceeded to teach Anna and Ruby the hustle. Once they had their moves down, they sauntered out for a night of dancing.

IT WAS OPENING NIGHT AT Faces, Murfreesboro's (or the 'Boro, as the locals called it) newest disco and bar, and people lined the sidewalk, waiting to get in. Ruby could hear the pulsating music as they walked up to the door. Sandy knew the bouncer so they walked past the crowd. To thank him, Sandy kissed the guy on his cheek, and then they entered the club.

A huge chandelier hung inside the foyer. The disco had been stylishly lit with multi-colored lights. They had two huge mirrored disco balls, which sparkled on an already crowded dance floor. The high-energy people who had made it inside were dancing, laughing and shouting to be heard over the loud jams that the DJ had cranked up.

Sandy grabbed Ruby and Anna and headed toward the dance floor. "Come on, my little darlings, let's boogie."

The girls danced all around with their arms waving in the air, moving to the beat. Ruby was having such a large time. It wasn't just the dancing—Ruby felt a special bond with best friends. The club periodically released fog along the floor, glitter floated from the ceiling and strobe lights had been set off in conjunction with the musical beats, to the squeals and delight of the clubbers. And it didn't take long for all three girls to be surrounded by guys, which added to the fun.

The girls danced to at least three more songs before they searched for a table. Anna found one close to the bar. Ruby plopped down onto a chair. Sandy flagged their waitress down to order drinks, only to learn a tall, blond man at the bar had bought their table a round. The girls thanked him with a wave and a nod.

Ruby took a sip and realized it was too tart for her taste. Sandy laughed, seeing Ruby wrinkle her nose, and said, "It's a Tequila Sunrise. If you don't want yours, sweetie, give it to me."

Ruby gave the drink to Sandy and ordered a Coke from the waitress. Marvin Gaye's "Got to Give it Up" began to play and Ruby jumped up. "Come on y'all! Let's dance, I love this song!"

Suddenly, someone grabbed her hand, and she turned to see Brent leading her onto the dance floor. Ruby peered back at Anna and Sandy and shrugged. Ruby wanted to dance. It was just a dance.

Looking at Brent under those lights and listening to the music reminded her of the fun times she had had with him this summer. She danced and moved rhythmically to the beat. He placed his hand on the small of her back, as they moved in perfect time. Ruby matched him, step for step. Their simple dance was quickly turning into something primal. She took a step back and let her hands drop away from his shoulders. Ruby began to dance by herself.

BRENT HAD BEEN SCANNING THE Faces crowd when he spotted Ruby with her friends. He had no idea she would be here tonight *and* without Reed. The moment he saw her, he felt a strange tightening in his chest. She looked so damn beautiful tonight in that dress, as he watched her and her friends hit the dance floor.

Brent had always thought Ruby was pretty, but tonight she was stunning. She took his breath away, her beauty shining like a brilliant star. Tonight she no longer had the look of a girl, but a beautiful woman.

He knew he had to have Ruby. She would not put him off any longer. He definitely didn't want Reed near her. Brent had been picking up girls left and right, just to keep his mind off Ruby. And then, he had seen her with Reed in the Italian restaurant and knew by the glow on her face, she was no longer a virgin.

Brent watched Ruby dance with her girlfriends. He had been making his way across the club, when he noticed the guy at the bar buying them drinks. He had seen the dude staring at Ruby. Brent quickly strode over to Ruby and grabbed her hand before the dude at the bar could make his move on her.

As they danced, her bare skin touched him, which knotted red-hot desire at the base of his spine. He didn't care about Reed or his friendship. All he cared about now was that Ruby was back in his arms. With her so close to him, his heart was pounding so loud it made his ears ring. He guided her away from the dance floor, and she continued dancing across the crowded room. He grabbed her hand and whirled her around to him. He dropped his arm around her waist, pulling her against the length of him and then rubbed his thumb gently across her cheek.

BRENT BENT OVER TO KISS Ruby, but she placed her hands on his chest and the smile on her face disappeared. "Don't, Brent. I'm sorry. I got carried away by the music. All I wanted to do was dance, for crying out loud."

Brent's eyes stayed steady on hers. He gently raised her wrist to his mouth and pressed a soft kiss there. "I don't want to stop. I miss you."

Ruby wriggled out of his grip, took a step back away from him, and frowned. "Stop it. I mean it. Behave yourself. I'm in love with Reed. I'm going back over to Anna and Sandy, now that my senses have returned."

Brent placed his hand against the wall to block her from moving. "He's not been faithful to you."

Ruby felt a spike in her chest. Her eyes flew up to meet his. She shouted, "You're lying. You're a damn liar!" She felt a nagging disillusionment, a sense of betrayal, just from hearing the words. Not her Reed. He was in love with her.

Brent stepped closer to her. He bent his head down to her, leaning close to her ear so she could hear him over the loud music. "I wasn't there in the flesh. I only heard about it. You know where there's smoke, there's fire." Then Brent leaned back against the wall of the club, crossing his arms against his chest.

Ruby didn't want to believe Reed would cheat on her, but now Brent had peaked her interest. She would not allow Brent to see her pain. Instead, she replied in a quick, clipped tone, "Well, you wanted my attention, now you have it."

Between the music and the people, it was hard for her to think, much less talk. Brent led her over to a table in the back of the club and they sat down. He pulled his chair close to her. "Reed's been seeing Tammy on the sly. Rachel and Patti live in the same apartment complex. Patti saw him come out of Tammy's apartment two days ago."

The colored lights and music Ruby had loved just moments ago were now making her nauseous. She shouted, "You're a liar! He drove to Knoxville two days ago." The music was ringing in her ears. Surely Reed wouldn't hurt her.

"What time did he leave?" Brent waved for the waitress, as he leaned closer to Ruby, placing his arm on the back of her chair.

"No, you tell me what time Patti was supposed to have seen him." Ruby's foot was tapping so fast on the floor it sounded like Morse code.

Brent lips were close to her ear, and she could feel his warm breath against her cheek. "Patti saw Reed come out of Tammy's apartment around lunch time. Patti was getting in her car when she saw Tammy wrap her arms around his neck and kiss him. Patti remembered Reed from the night we saw you guys at Tony's."

The waitress came over and asked, "May I take your order?" She smiled at Brent, leaning over to show her cleavage and Ruby rolled her eyes.

Brent said, "Two whiskeys and a couple of Cokes on the side, please."

Ruby lowered her face into her hands and began to cry. She thought Brent was lying, but Reed had left her house at eleven. The timeline was there. Brent placed his hand on her shoulder, but she brushed it off.

"Why did you tell me this, Brent? Do you hate me so much? Do you love to hurt me?" Ruby wiped away her tears with the back of her hand.

The dance floor was shoulder to shoulder with people. Sandy danced with the man who had bought them a round from the bar. She spotted Ruby, sitting with Brent, and was making her way across the floor to her.

Brent leaned back in his chair and then threw his hands up in frustration. "Hell, no, I hated telling you. But you deserve the truth, whether or not you ever go out with me again." The waitress set the drinks on the table and Brent paid for them.

Ruby reached over, grabbed the whiskey and drained the glass. She blinked her eyes several times and then chased the whiskey with Coke. Ruby's stomach had flipped several times when Brent said Reed had kissed Tammy. How could Reed? When the waitress passed by again, Ruby touched her arm and said, "Bring me another whiskey, please."

Brent swore under his breath. "Ruby, don't do that. You don't need another whiskey. You rarely drink alcohol." Ruby nodded to the waitress in the affirmative; the waitress nodded and left their table.

Ruby threw her head back and laughed loudly. Anger began to hotly surge in her veins. "Oh, Brent, sure I do. Don't you want me drunk? I'll be easy, isn't that what you want?" Ruby rested her forearms on the table with her fingers linked together and twirled her thumbs.

Brent shook his head sadly and covered her hands with his. "I shouldn't have told you about Reed. I see that now. Maybe it was innocent."

"Oh, now that's rich, really rich. You're taking up for him." Ruby couldn't believe Brent was actually taking up for Reed. It was ludicrous.

The waitress set down the whiskey. Ruby looked up to the waitress and then pointed to Brent. "He's got it, and he's paying for all of my drinks tonight. As a matter of fact, just start us a tab, honey." Ruby picked up the whiskey and drained another shot. The warm liquid rushed down her throat and she instantly relaxed. At least her hands weren't shaking anymore.

Damn Reed, he had seen Tammy. He had been inside her apartment minutes after leaving her to go to Knoxville. She remembered seeing the strain in his eyes the morning he left and thought it was there because of his mother. Ruby guessed it was stressful stringing two girls along at the same time. She intended on getting blind, stinking drunk.

Sandy joined them at the table. "What the hell are you doing, Ruby? I've been watching you, missy. That's the second drink you've shot in less than fifteen minutes. You're going to be drunk and sick. I don't like cleaning up puke." The club had gotten so crowded that people were standing behind their table or walking past their chairs, bumping into them occasionally.

"Okay, Mom. Aren't you the one who's always telling me to let loose?" Ruby was so mad, the sides of her hands tingled. She wanted to punch somebody, and punch them hard. Maybe Tammy would actually show up tonight, and she could beat the living crap out of her. Just visualizing kicking Tammy's ass made her laugh again. Brent and Sandy both looked at her like she had lost her mind.

Sandy narrowed her eyes at Brent. "What did you do, slip her a mickey?"

"Hell, no, I didn't slip her anything." Brent placed his hand on Ruby's thigh.

Ruby pushed Brent's hand away and then started rolling with laughter so hard that tears were streaming down her cheeks. "He didn't slip me anything, but the truth."

Anna walked over to the table and pulled a chair up beside Ruby.

"What the heck is going on over here?"

Brent was practically yelling to be heard over the crowd and music. "It's my fault. Patti saw Reed come out of Tammy's the day he left for Knoxville."

Anna's and Sandy's heads shot up at his revelation. They both looked at Ruby like their dog had just died.

Ruby wasn't going to sit here and let the news of Reed's infidelity ruin her night. She stood up, swayed just a little, but then braced herself on Brent's shoulder. "I want to dance. I wanna dance all night long. Come on, life's short and then you get screwed!" Her laughter continued as she danced her way back to the floor, while Brent, Sandy and Anna followed her.

Sandy punched Brent in the arm. "You're such an asshole. Why did you have to tell her? Did you think by telling her about Reed, it would change her mind about you?"

Brent, Anna and Sandy were dancing together. He just looked at Sandy and shrugged, while he kept his eye on Ruby.

Ruby twirled her dress around and then closed her eyes as she got into the groove of the music. She danced with her hands in the air. A guy on the dance floor could see Ruby didn't have a partner so he came up behind Ruby and circled his arm around her waist. He pulled her next to him. Ruby didn't even turn to see who it was; she just danced next to him, provocatively.

Brent stepped in between the guy and Ruby. "Back off, dude, if you know what's good for you." The guy looked at Brent's size, turned, and went looking for another girl.

Ruby moved her hips back and forth, pressing against Brent. She felt his muscles tighten as she ran her fingers over his chest. She reached up, placing her arms around his neck and whispered into his ear, "Do you want me, Brent? Do you want to make love to me tonight?" She ran her tongue around his ear and he covered her mouth with his.

Brent dropped his arm around her waist and shifted his angle to press kisses on her neck and then brushed his lips across her cheek. "Yes, sweet girl, I want to make love to you tonight." As they danced, he pushed his knee in between her legs and they moved back and forth in slow circles with his hand resting on her bum.

When the song ended, Ruby said, "Let's blow this taco stand."

Ruby grabbed his hand and headed for the door.

Sandy ran up behind Ruby, grabbing her arm, and jerked her around. "Don't do this, Ruby. You don't know what really happened with Reed. Don't leave with Brent."

"I know all I need to." Ruby turned to Brent. "Do you still have keys to your grandparent's cabin at the lake?"

"Yes, I do. You want to go to the cabin?" He kissed the back of her hand.

"Yes, I do. I need to get the hell out of this town." Satisfied with her decision, she said to Sandy, "Reed is coming home tomorrow. Tell him I'm out of town. I need to make some decisions before I talk to him again."

Sandy frowned at Ruby. "I won't make promises I can't keep. You're drunk and making a big mistake, girlie. I'll remind you later what an idiot you're being tonight."

Ruby lifted one shoulder toward Sandy. "Suit yourself." Ruby looked back to Brent. "Let's ride, Clyde."

Ruby started out the door when Anna ran up to her. "Ruby, are you sure about this? You love Reed, and I know he loves you." Anna hugged her tightly.

"Anna, honestly, I'm not sure about anything, except that I want to get the hell out of Dodge. I'll see you tomorrow, sometime. Love you."

Anna replied, "Love you more.

Chapter 11

Get Away

RUBY HAD BRENT STOP BY her house on Bell Street to pick up some clothes. She quickly changed into jeans and sweatshirt and then grabbed the overnight bag she normally used when she spent the night with Reed.

Reed—how long had he been seeing Tammy? Had he ever stopped?

Ruby's head was swimming from the accusations and the alcohol. On the way to Centerhill, they stopped by the all-night store for groceries. After they had Brent's car packed, he pulled onto Highway 96 toward Centerhill Lake.

Ruby gazed out the window, her head in a fog as they passed farmland and subdivisions. Her mind kept playing over the day Reed had left for Knoxville. She remembered making love to him early in the morning and kissing him before he pulled out of the driveway. But instead of driving straight to Knoxville, he had taken a detour to Tammy's. Ruby brushed a tear away with her shoulder.

As the car climbed elevation, Ruby's ears began to pop. Ruby's head had started aching. But it wasn't her head that caused her the real pain. Nothing could stop the pain in her heart, because she was desperately in love with Reed. Ruby tossed a glance at Brent. Crap, she had told him she would sleep with him.

Brent handed her a bottle of aspirin. "Go ahead and take a couple of these before your head gets worse. Let me know if you think you're going to be sick."

Ruby took the aspirin bottle and popped a couple in her mouth. She drank down some Coke to swallow them. "Brent, do you still love me?"

His hands gripped the steering wheel hard as the muscles flexed in his biceps. He glanced at her and then back to the road. "I never stopped, Ruby."

Ruby didn't believe him or Reed. She wouldn't be surprised at all to find out they were still playing the damn *Tap It* game. She had been an idiot and fell over the cliffs in love for the hot and pretty damn scrumptious Reed Jackson. She was still crazy about him. But Brent and Reed were too much alike to be faithful. She didn't love Brent. She should be feeling guilty for using Brent. She should feel guilty for being here with him. But didn't because she was too mad.

Halfway to the cabin, Ruby began to think maybe this had been a bad idea. It seemed like a great idea when the whiskey had been talking. "Brent, I'm sorry, but I want to go home. Will you take me back home?"

Brent left one hand on the steering wheel and the other squeezed her thigh. "I'll take you home, honey, if you really want to go. You're safe with me, sweet girl. I want to make love to you, but I'm vain enough to want you to love me back. Let's drive up, no strings attached. I'm just happy you're here with me. The leaves will be beautiful this time of year over the lake."

Tears threatened to spill over her cheeks. "I don't want to hurt you, but you deserve the truth, too. No matter what Reed has done, I still love him. I'm just so mad and hurt, I didn't really think about how it would affect you. I'm being selfish. Thank you for understanding and for telling me. I mean it. I'm glad you told me about Reed."

He reached over and held her hand. "I'll always be here for you, baby girl."

THE CAR SPIRALED UP THE winding, wooded driveway of the cabin, and Brent parked in front of the garage. They got out of the car and walked to the trunk. Ruby picked up her bag and Brent grabbed the groceries.

The cabin had been built in the early '70s and was surrounded by dense woods. It had a wrap-around deck with rocking chairs that overlooked the lake. As she walked inside, she glanced up at the loft ceiling, which had exposed crossbeams running the length of the cabin. Ruby walked through the den, passing through the kitchen before walking into the master bedroom with her overnight bag. Brent's grandfather loved duck hunting, so the cabin was filled with framed duck art, and he had several prize ducks, stuffed and hanging on the walls.

Ruby walked back into the great room and joined Brent in the kitchen. She helped him put away the groceries in the fridge and cabinets. In the den, one wall was dedicated to the rock fireplace with a solid oak mantle. The wood bin was full of cedar logs. Brent started a fire, while she sat on the couch. She wondered what would have happened between Brent and her had she never met Reed. Would she still be with him? Would he have been the one she made love to?

Brent walked over and rustled her hair. "Hey, kiddo, don't look so gloomy. Things always happen for a reason. Everything will be okay in the end. You want some hot chocolate?"

Ruby smoothed her hair out of her face and then stood. She walked to the fireplace and stretched her hands out to feel the warmth from the blaze. "Sure. I can make it if you give me the ingredients."

Brent loosely slung his arm around her shoulder and pulled her away from the fireplace as they walked back into the kitchen. "Let's make it together."

In the kitchen, Brent set out the cocoa, sugar, vanilla, milk and marshmallows. "Hey, look under the stove and pull out a small pan."

Ruby opened the kitchen cabinets and rummaged through the pots until she found one she thought was suitable. "Will this work?" He nodded yes.

Ruby pulled the drawers out and found the utensils and then she measured out the sugar and then the cocoa and mixed the ingredients together, adding milk and stirring occasionally.

Brent chuckled watching her. "It looks like you've made that a time or two."

"I love hot chocolate." Ruby kept stirring until the hot chocolate began to steam.

Brent walked back into the den and turned the stereo on. He added one more log to the crackling fire and stoked the logs with the fire iron. He walked back into the kitchen to join Ruby. He pulled two mugs out of the cabinet and then he sat at the kitchen counter watching her.

Ruby began to feel a little better about being up here alone with Brent. She loved this cabin. They had had fun up here last summer. Ruby poured the steaming hot chocolate into the mugs over the stainless steel sink. There was a window over the sink, which looked over the lake. Brent had flipped on the back porch light and she could see snow flurries floating in the air.

Ruby turned to Brent and grinned. "It's snowing." He jumped down from the counter and peeked out the window, placing his hand on her side. Tingles shot up her spine.

"Yep, it's snowing. It won't stick, but it's nice to look at, isn't it?" He placed a light kiss on her cheek.

They sat in front of the fireplace, on the couch. Ruby kicked off her tennis shoes and crossed her legs. She held the mug in her hands and took sips of hot chocolate while she stared into the hypnotic fire. The night had emotionally drained her. The warmth of the hot chocolate and the fire made her sleepy. Brent placed his arm around her. Ruby sat her cup on the table and leaned back against his shoulder.

"You can go to sleep, sweet girl. I'll be here when you wake up." Brent stroked her hair and she drifted off to sleep.

RUBY STOOD INSIDE THE OLD Methodist church that sat on top of Campbell Ridge. The church had been built in the late 1800s. It had a wooden lectern and pews. The stained glass windows cast warm golds and reds across the sanctuary. The double doors at the entrance of the church were wide open as the brilliant sunlight streaked inside the foyer. As she walked to the entrance, she noticed a few hymnals that had been tossed on the seats of the empty pews.

Ruby had never attended this church. The congregation had

moved in the middle 1960s to a more modern building, but Ruby had always loved this old church building more, because it was homey.

As Ruby neared the opening, Reed came up behind her and caught her hand. A beautiful little girl ran up to her and said, "Mama and Daddy, can we go for ice cream, today? Please, please, please?"

Ruby studied the little girl's face. She was a pretty little thing, with Reed's dark brown hair and eyes. Ruby placed her hand lightly on the girl's shoulder. "Well first, young lady, I think you need to give your Mama a kiss, don't you?"

The little girl stretched her arms out wide to be picked up. Ruby picked her up and gave her a kiss. She held the child in her arms. Reed held out his hands, and the little girl went from Ruby into his arms. He kissed the little girl, and she placed her head on Reed's shoulder. Ruby, Reed and their daughter walked into the sunlight and disappeared.

Ruby sat up quickly and looked around the cabin. Brent had fallen asleep. He had his legs stretched out and his head lay back on the couch cushion. She stood up and walked over to the fireplace, picked up the poker, and stirred the logs to a blaze. She added one more log to the fire and stared into the flames.

Ruby had life and death dreams. Her life dreams were always about a pregnancy. Her death dreams coincided with the passing of someone she loved. Tonight, she had dreamed about her own child. She placed her hand over her abdomen.

Ruby had been on the pill all summer. Was she pregnant? How could she be pregnant? She knew one girl who had gotten pregnant on the pill. Her high school friend Cathy had been on the pill for two years when she had gotten pregnant with her daughter, Becky. Becky was now three and so precocious.

The sweet little girl in Ruby's dream looked like her Reed. Ruby ached for Reed. How could Reed hurt her so by being with Tammy?

Ruby quietly walked into the kitchen. The time on the stove said five o'clock. She didn't want to wake Brent. She grabbed her coat and walked through the master bedroom door and onto the deck.

Ruby stood on the deck, drinking in the view across the lake as the sunrise kissed the horizon. The sun was a crimson red as it faded out into the palest pink, spilling across the sky. She wondered what would happen the next time she saw Reed. When she did see him again, he needed to tell her the truth about Tammy. He needed to make up his mind, one way or the other.

She had had lingering doubts about his fidelity after seeing him with Tammy in the bookstore. She should have asked him then. To his credit, when Reed was asked a direct question he told the truth. But, right this minute, she would believe anything he said, if they could only go back to the way things were only a few days ago.

Brent walked out onto the deck. "You okay?"

"No, I'm not okay. But, like you said, things happen for a reason. Dawn approaches, and a new day begins. I'm not going to be able to sleep, but don't let me stop you. I'm fine. I'm thinking." Ruby looked back out over the lake.

He placed his hand on her shoulder. "Would it bother you if I stay with you while you think?" The stars above them had all but faded as the sky turned a pale blue.

She turned to face him. Ruby could see the longing in his eyes. His piercing green eyes stared back at her and her stomach flipped. "No, I don't mind if you stay. I would like some coffee, please."

Brent leaned over and kissed her lightly on the lips. "Sure thing." He walked back inside the cabin.

Ruby watched as the sun rose higher in the sky, casting streaks of sunlight through the russet and gold leaves of the trees. The water on the lake was like a sheet of black glass this morning and the fog below the cliff was beginning to lift. She felt cocooned, protected and isolated from the realities of the world.

Brent handed her a cup of coffee and smiled at her. He had remembered how she liked it. She placed the mug on the rail and then placed her hand over his and squeezed it. "Thank you, Brent."

He let his hand drop away and went back into the kitchen to grab his mug. He returned to stand beside her, took a drink, and then said, "Are you cold? I could get you a blanket."

"No, I'm fine. You have been good to me. I don't deserve it." She took another sip of coffee.

Ruby heard a car engine. Someone was pulling into the cabin's driveway. Brent heard it, too. She said, "Do you think it's your grandparents?"

"Maybe."

They both turned to see Reed and Sandy walking swiftly around the corner of the cabin's wraparound porch. Reed stormed out onto the deck. "What in the hell do you think you're doing, bringing her up here?" Reed stood an inch from Brent. His chest was heaving with deep breaths. He didn't even look at Ruby.

Brent dropped his mug on the deck and pushed Ruby behind him. Brent went into a boxing stance as he readied himself for a fight. "I'm protecting her from you!"

Reed clenched his fists at his sides and took one more step closer to Brent. His voice shook with fury. "You have exactly five seconds to move away from her."

Brent spread his legs slightly farther apart. The muscles in his biceps flexed for a fight. "You have no right to be here. She came here with me, *willingly*."

Ruby stepped between them. "Stop it, you two, please stop it. I don't want the two of you fighting again." Ruby tossed a perturbed glance over her shoulder to Sandy, and said, "Thanks a lot."

Sandy crossed the deck to stand beside her. "I did this for your own good. Reed came to the house an hour ago. He drove like a bat out of hell to get here."

Ruby turned her back to Reed and Sandy and then gently placed her hand against Brent's cheek. "Please go inside with Sandy. I want to talk to Reed, okay?"

Brent kissed her hand and then looked over Ruby's shoulders as he glared at Reed, and when he looked back to her, his expression softened. "I will do anything for you, sweet girl." He bumped Reed's shoulder hard as he walked by him.

Reed grabbed Brent's shirt, pulling him an inch from his face. "I will kill you if I find out you have touched her."

Brent jerked out of Reed's grip. "Get your damn hands off me. Ask her yourself. I'm honorable. That's more than I can say for you."

Ruby stepped between them again. "Stop it, you two. Please go inside, Brent." Turning to Sandy she said, "You, too. Please go inside with Brent."

Reed's hands shook and he was breathing hard. He closed his eyes and counted aloud to ten, took a breath and said, "I can't believe you came up here with him."

Ruby exploded with anger as she shouted at him, "I'd say that's the pot calling the kettle black. What about you? You—You hooked up with Tammy before you left for Knoxville?"

Reed grabbed Ruby by the shoulders. "Are you going to listen to me?"

Ruby eased out of Reed's hold, walked to the porch swing, and motioned for him to sit beside her. "Please, I'm all ears."

"Tammy called me while you were in the shower. I didn't tell you because I knew you would be furious. Her grandmother died. She was as close to her as you are with your grandfather. Tammy and I are friends. I only stopped by her place for about fifteen minutes, before I left, to offer my condolences. I saw Patti and knew she'd tell Brent. I just didn't think Brent had the balls to tell you. It was nothing."

Ruby's face was in full flush. "You've got to be kidding me. You go to your old girlfriend's place and you're seen kissing Tammy, and that's nothing?" She gripped the porch swing's arm.

Reed twisted in the seat to face her and tried to caress her face with his hand, but she shoved him away. "It was nothing. I didn't kiss her back."

Ruby wanted to scream, but instead she stood up and stomped her foot. "You knew I would be mad, but you did it anyway. A phone call to Tammy offering your condolences would have been sufficient. You should have told me, whether I got mad or not. Or you could have taken me with you. I would have understood. But instead you went inside her apartment behind my back! You were in her arms and you kissed her! I'm so dad blame mad at you, I can't see straight!"

Reed stood and pulled her into his arms. "I'm sorry. I shouldn't have gone over there without telling you first. But that doesn't *excuse* you from coming up here with him! Did you kiss him to get back at me? Please tell me you didn't sleep with him."

Ruby looked up into his eyes and her throat choked with emotion. Her voice quivered, "O ye of little faith." He tried to wipe her tears away. "Don't touch me, Reed. You've ripped me apart. I've had a miserable night because of you."

Reed plopped down on a deck chair and cradled his face in his hands. "I'm in love with you, Ruby, only you."

"And I only love you." Her shoulders slumped as her heart broke into tiny pieces and she walked to the railing, looking out over the lake. The sun was up and it warmed her face. There was a fishing boat racing across the channel.

Reed went to stand beside her. He placed his hand inside his pocket and pulled out a jewelry box, twirling it over in his hand. "I should have asked you sooner. I left my home in East Tennessee at midnight and drove straight to your house. I knew I wanted to marry you for a while. Honestly, I've been fighting myself over loving you. I've been so afraid of committing to anyone, and then you came along and I wanted to change. Watching my parents over the past couple of days and seeing how much they love each other, I knew that's what we have and I didn't want to waste another minute. I couldn't drive fast enough to get back to you. When I knocked on your door, Sandy answered, and before I could crawl in your bed, she stopped me." His face was getting red and he pointed toward the kitchen. "She told me about you and him!"

Ruby drew in her breath, seeing the jewelry box in his hand. She steadied her hands on the railing and stared up at him. He was staring out at the lake. He looked good, even in a disheveled state.

Reed turned, grabbed her hand, and placed the jewelry box in it, awaiting a reply. "I want to marry you. I want to spend my life with you. I want you to be my wife, if you'll have me."

Ruby opened up the jewelry box and found a white gold and diamond engagement ring. Tears sprang into her eyes as she slipped the ring on her finger. She smiled up at Reed and said, "It fits. How did you know what size to get?"

He looked down at her, with a sideways grin. "I slipped a string around your finger while you were sleeping. Is that a yes?"

Ruby shoulder-bumped him. "Yes, but this doesn't mean you're out of the dog house."

Reed pulled her into his arms and rested his forehead against hers. "So, may I kiss you now?"

She stood on tiptoe and put her arms around his neck and kissed him soundly.

BRENT AND SANDY LOOKED ON from the sliding glass doors. Sandy placed her arm around Brent's waist. "Well, you did give it the old college try. Come on. Let's get a cup of coffee." She walked over to the coffee pot, saying, "You know, Brent, you're a really good dancer." Brent followed Sandy to the kitchen with his eyes glued to her butt.

Chapter 12
Oh Girl

RUBY SAT CLOSE TO REED on the drive back to Murfreesboro. There was a wintry chill in the air and the promise of snow lurked in the late October sky. The two-lane highway had double yellow lines with no shoulder. As they approached the stretch of the road called Dead Man's Curve, Ruby looked up a second too late to see a deer run out of the woods and dart into the highway in front of Reed's car.

"Reed, watch out!" she screamed.

Reed was driving too fast to react and tried slamming on his brakes, but he hit the deer. That was when everything seemed to happen in slow motion. Ruby heard the brakes screech, and she could smell burning rubber. She heard the violent crunch of metal as the car skidded in the gravel toward the ditch. She felt as if they were slowly floating through the air—and then, all at once, everything sped up, as Ruby heard the deafening grind of metal, and the car flipped on its side. Ruby's head hit the windshield, and then there was nothing.

REED WOKE TO A COPPERY taste in his mouth and the smell of burnt rubber and antifreeze. His head ached with intense pain. It took about a second for him to remember what had happened. He looked down and found Ruby pinned underneath him. His car was flipped over on the passenger side. A surge of adrenaline pumped through his body as he lifted himself off Ruby and gently shook her.

Reed lifted her from the floorboard and held her in his arms. "Ruby, honey, wake up. Are you okay?" There was no movement from her. He screamed, "Ruby, honey, can you hear me? Please wake up, Ruby!" His hands shook as he felt for her pulse. *Thank you, sweet Jesus! She's alive!*

Reed heard people screaming outside his car. There must have been at least a dozen people at the scene. He heard sirens in the distance as people approached the car.

Brent yelled, "Reed, help is coming! We're going to try and place the car upright. Can you hold on to something?"

Reed braced himself with one arm so he would not fall on Ruby. With his other arm, he tried to secure her next to him, gently, so she wouldn't hit the dash when the others flipped the car upright.

Brent hollered, "On the count of three: One! Two! Three!"

The car flipped upright and bounced like a buggy while Reed gently cradled Ruby in his arms.

Brent opened the driver's side door and started to pull Reed out. Reed screamed, "Wait!! I'm not leaving Ruby! Has anyone called an ambulance?"

Reed glanced up to see the distraught look on Brent's face when Brent first noticed Ruby. And then Brent fell backwards, nearly falling down. Ruby lay unconscious, nearly lifeless in Reed's arms.

Brent regained his balance by placing his hand on the roof of the car, and his voice quivered, "Reed, I can see the ambulance lights now. The state trooper is here...you're bleeding pretty badly."

Reed was on the brink of hysteria. "Brent, I don't care! I'm staying here with her."

Someone handed Brent a couple of blankets. Reed noticed Brent's hands were shaking, too, when he handed Reed the blankets. Brent said, "You need to place this over Ruby and one around you. The paramedics are here now."

The paramedics were equipped with two gurneys, one for Reed and the other for Ruby. Minutes later the paramedics were pulling Reed from the car. He begged, "Please get Ruby first. I'm okay. Get Ruby out of the car." Reed was out of his mind when he tried to punch one the paramedics as they were pulling him from the wreckage. He screamed and cried out, "Ruby! I'm here, darling! I'm not leaving you, baby! I'm right here!"

Ruby was still unconscious.

RUBY WOKE TO THE WONDERFUL aroma of homemade apple pie and music from the 1940s playing on the radio. She blinked her eyes several times. She was in George and Lizzie's cabin, but somehow it looked different. It looked like the old family photo that hung in the great room at Everglade Farms. Ruby was lying on the couch in the breezeway. There was an old rotator fan blowing on her from her granddaddy's old desk.

That's so weird. She thought the desk was in her mama's house.

A warm breeze flowed through the cabin. This place didn't seem real, as if she was in a dream, but she could feel the breeze blow against her skin, and it felt like love, surrounding her, embracing her in comfort.

A minute later, a woman in an ankle-length, navy blue dress with white polka dots sat down beside her. She resembled Ruby.

The woman asked, "Ruby, do you feel better?"

Ruby answered, "I feel fine. Do I smell homemade apple pie? It smells just like my mama's cooking. Is she here?"

The woman answered, "No, child. She isn't here. You're here to rest for a spell. Then you can go back home."

Ruby said, "Is this George's cabin?"

The woman held Ruby's hand. "This place is what you want it to be, Ruby. You must feel disoriented. I did too, the first time I came here. It will be all right."

The lady stood and grabbed a cloth from a bowl of water. Then she wrung out the excess water and placed it on Ruby's forehead. "I'm your grandmother, Ruby. Your grandmother on the Campbell side."

Utterly befuddled, Ruby said, "But, you're dead."

The little girl from her previous dream ran into the room. She looked at the old woman and smiled. Then she hopped on the couch next to Ruby. "Hi, Mama, are you feeling better?"

Ruby looked perplexed at the beautiful child. "Why are you calling me Mama, honey?"

The little girl giggled, and said, "Well, silly goose, because you are. I know you're a little confused about this place, but it's going to be okay. I want you to remember me when you get back."

Ruby said, "Get back where?"

The little girl said, "Back home to Daddy. He's very sad right now. He misses you." Ruby looked around. "Where am I?"

The little girl said, "This is the in-between. You and Daddy were in a car wreck. You're hurt right now. That's why you can see me. You dreamed about me, remember? I'm your baby."

The little girl climbed into Ruby's lap. "I was in the accident, too, but I was too small to survive. I wanted to visit with you now, in the in-between, so when you go back, you won't be sad. I'll always be here waiting for you, Mama, when you come back home again, for good. You feel all the love here? The love here never goes away. Just like my love for you and Daddy. It'll never go away. Remember, you and Daddy have been given a very precious gift. True love is very precious. Cherish each other, always, as I will cherish you both for eternity."

Ruby was amazed at her little girl who spoke like an adult. Ruby was totally confused, but didn't feel sad. She only felt love for this precious child who sat in her lap. Ruby touched the child's cheek and asked, "What's your name, precious?"

The little girl looked up at her and smiled. "Alisa"

Ruby's grandmother went over and closed the shutters on the windows. "Honey, why don't you take a nap? You'll feel better when you wake up."

Ruby stretched back out on the couch, with Alisa in her arms, and quickly fell asleep.

THE PARAMEDICS PULLED RUBY FROM the wreckage after they placed a brace around her neck to secure it. They removed her from the car carefully as Reed watched from his gurney and frantically begged to know her condition.

Reed said, "Is she okay? Please tell me she's okay!"

The paramedic said, "Sir, you have to let us do our job. We'll take care of her first and then move on to you, but you must sit still on the gurney. You're bleeding."

They carried Ruby on the gurney and lifted her up into the ambulance. They had radioed the hospital and they instructed the paramedic to immediately start an IV, and arranged an echocardiogram monitor and oxygen.

A paramedic came back to Reed and asked, "Sir, what is your name?"

Reed replied, "I'm Reed Harley Jackson and that's my fiancée, Ruby Jane Glenn."

The paramedic said, "Sir, I need you to please lie back. We have to get you in the ambulance."

Once Reed was in the ambulance, he propped himself up on an elbow and looked over at Ruby. The paramedic had cleaned the blood from her face. She was so pale, and that made Reed cry.

The paramedic said, "Mr. Jackson, I am going to start you on an IV."

Reed noticed blood oozing from between Ruby's legs. He was on the verge of passing out and he tried to speak, but all he could do was point toward Ruby's legs. The paramedic turned and quickly adjusted her IV and began to place pads to soak up the heavy vaginal bleeding. Then Ruby's blood pressure bottomed out, and the paramedic began doing chest compressions on Ruby.

The driver sped along the highway and radioed again to the hospital. "We have a code 226, six minutes until arrival. Be ready for us."

Reed began hyperventilating. "She's dead?"

The paramedic calmly addressed Reed. "Mr. Jackson, please remain calm."

With a nod, Reed began to talk to Ruby in a quivering voice and said, "Ruby, honey, I need you. You can't leave me. Can you hear me? I need you. You fight for me. I love you, Ruby Jane, please don't leave me."

The ambulance ploughed through red lights, weaving in and out of traffic, and turned on Bell Street heading to the ER entrance. The paramedic ripped opened a package and held the needle for the injection. Reed sucked in his breath and passed out the moment the needle entered her heart.

BRENT AND SANDY WATCHED AS the ambulance flew toward Murfreesboro. Sandy was crying as they walked back to his car. Brent stopped and held her in the circle of his arms. "Sandy, we have to go to the ER. I'll call Reed's parents, and you'll have to call Ruby's family."

Sandy tried to stop crying. She inhaled three quick breaths, then said, "Oh, Brent, I'm afraid. Ruby looked so pale. Ruby's my best friend in the whole wide world. I don't know what I'll do if something happens to her."

RUBY WOKE AGAIN, BUT THIS time she was on the top of Campbell Ridge, standing next to her favorite old oak tree. The sky was a vivid blue and light radiated all around her, but there was no sun. She walked through the open pasture full of wildflowers—purple sage, African daisies, snapdragons, and sweet William rustled in the warm gentle breeze. She walked around the oak tree to the edge of the cliff that overlooked a vast river, flowing with the same gentle rhythm of the breeze. Ruby thought it odd because Everglade Farms had a creek, and not a river.

The landscape across the lazy hills gave her a peace beyond any understanding. She walked toward the river, down the rocky crags, stepping carefully so she wouldn't slip and fall. The pebbled sandstone crunched under her bare feet, but she felt no pain.

A big boulder jutted out over the river. She climbed up, looking over the rock to watch the water rush through the riverbed. Ruby sat down on the big rock, letting her legs dangle over the edge. She wore a long white muslin dress with quarter-length sleeves, so soft, it felt like silk over her skin.

A man walked up and sat down beside her, his radiance so brilliant she should have been shielding her eyes, but didn't. His light illuminated out from the white robe he wore. "Hi, Ruby."

"Hello." She could feel the positive energy emitting from him. She said, "I know who you are—you're the messenger I saw in the cave when I was fifteen, the one in my dreams. Holy moly, may I touch you?"

He grinned and she could feel his energy radiating through her, the rocks and the river. It was if he were the sun. His energy hummed like a whole hive of bumblebees. "My dear, that's why I love you. You're so inquisitive." He reached out his hand toward her and she caught his hand in hers. It was the most indescribable but wonderful feeling. If she could only hold on for a little while longer, she would be able to see and know all life's secrets. He was bright and beautiful.

His eyes were full of love, knowledge and compassion. Ruby asked, "Who are you? What are you? Do you have a name? Why did you choose Anna, Sandy and me for the gifts? Why stones? And why am I here?"

He smiled. "Ruby, you have a choice to make. You may move forward, and I will be happy to answer all your questions. Or you may go back. If you choose to go back, then you will have the answers you seek in time." He continued holding her hand.

"That's not fair. Tell me something? Anything?" she pleaded.

"My name is Seneca. Now, what is your choice, Ruby?"

"That's easy. I want to go back. I'm in love with Reed. We're getting married."

In an instant, the radiant man, the messenger named Seneca, was gone.

THE PARAMEDICS OPENED THE DOORS of the ambulance. There were two medical teams waiting, one for Ruby and the other one for Reed ready to take them inside the ER.

REED WOKE UP IN A hospital room. His father, Donald, stood up from his chair and went to stand by his son's side. Reed's mom was still recuperating from her emergency surgery. Reed was disoriented as he looked around the hospital room. The light over his bed was turned on, and the blinds were closed. His head was killing him. He bolted upright in the bed and searing pain shot through his rib cage.

Reed looked at his dad. "How's Ruby? Is she okay?"

Donald Jackson held his son's hand. "Reed, lie back down. You have several broken ribs. Ruby's still unconscious in the intensive care unit. She has a great medical team working tirelessly, trying to help her. I spoke with her father, Harry, and he promised me when he had news, he would tell us. You need to rest, son."

Reed didn't want to lie down. He wanted to see Ruby. He swung his legs over the side of the bed. "I need to see her. Dad, she died in the ambulance. I saw her die! Help me see her, please."

"Reed, I promise she is still alive and breathing. From what I hear from her family, your Ruby is a scrapper. I'll go and see if someone in the family can help you to get into her room. I'll be back soon."

SANDY AND ANNA WALKED OVER to Ruby's father in the ICU waiting room. Sandy looked up at him and asked, "Mr. Glenn, do you think it's possible for Anna and me to see Ruby? I mean, uh, alone?"

Harry shoved his hand in his coat pocket and gave the girls a half smile. "I don't see what harm it would do. Come on."

Anna intended to use her healing ability to help Ruby. She had discussed it with Sandy. They needed to be alone with her for a few minutes. The healing energy in the past had only taken several minutes.

Harry buzzed the door to the ICU, and a nurse opened the double doors. "Hi, Mr. Glenn." She glanced at Anna and Sandy and then back to Harry.

With a shrug, he said, "They're sisters." Harry watched as the nurse ushered the girls down the corridor.

Inside Ruby's room, Lee Glenn stood. "Girls, I'm so glad you're here." She crossed over and gave a hug to Anna and then one to Sandy.

Sandy placed a hand on Lee's shoulder. "Mrs. Glenn, why don't you go get something to eat or just walk a bit? It'll do you good. We'll stay with Ruby." Lee nodded and told the girls thank you and left the room.

Sandy looked out Ruby's door and then closed it behind her.

"Okay, Anna, do your stuff."

Anna felt the energy surging through her as she placed her hands over Ruby. She looked over to Sandy and said, "Hold her hand, Sandy." Anna placed her hands over Ruby's lower abdomen and then moved her hands over Ruby's heart.

Anna didn't stop until her hands rested on the top of Ruby's head. She tingled from head to toe as the buzzing energy coursed through her hands. Anna closed her eyes and let the energy continued surging through her. She felt as though her fingers were the prongs of an electrical cord stuck into an outlet, and then the hospital experienced a power surge. Anna held onto her friend for a few more minutes as Ruby's nurse rushed into the room. Anna's energy left and Ruby opened her eyes.

The nurse looked from Anna to Ruby and asked in disbelief, "What did you do to her?"

Anna offered the nurse the easiest explanation. "I healed her. Ruby is awake. You need to go get her doctor." The nurse opened her mouth to say something, but then closed it. She left the room, shaking her head, and closed the door behind her. From Anna's healing experience with her mom, she felt sure the nurse would never remember the healing episode.

Anna walked over to Ruby, placing her hand on Ruby's battered face, and thankfully, Ruby was wide awake. "How do you feel?"

Ruby looked over to Sandy and then back to Anna. She blinked a couple of times and then said, "I feel fine. You healed me?" Anna nodded.

Ruby cleared her voice and said, "I met the messenger in my dreams. His name is Seneca. I died in the ambulance and I went to this unbelievable, mystical place. I recognized him, but not from the carving. I just knew it was him. It was like I was clairvoyant or something. He was radiant and beautiful beyond words. I had a choice to move on to a better place or come back. I chose to come back. I wanted to come back to Reed."

Sandy lifted Ruby's hand and kissed it. "I'm so glad you came back, sister."

Ruby's smile lit up the room. "I'm pretty sure Seneca wanted me to come back. I asked him all sorts of questions, and he said time would reveal all my answers. And then poof, he was gone and I was back here."

Anna and Sandy were grinning at Ruby when Harry and Lee rushed in the room. Sandy hugged Harry and said, "She's okay. Ruby is okay."

DONALD WALKED OUT OF REED'S hospital room and down the corridor to the elevators. As he got on the elevator, he thought about Reed. What if Ruby didn't make it? How in the world would he tell his son?

Two nurses joined him on the elevator. They were chatting about what they were doing after work. Donald stepped out on the first floor and walked toward the ICU waiting room. He looked inside and didn't recognize anyone, when Harry, Ruby's dad, walked out the ICU double doors.

Donald walked over to Harry and asked, "Any news?"

He slapped Donald on the back and said, "Ruby's awake and she is okay. The doctor said Ruby's vitals are stable. Her brain activity is normal, and thankfully no swelling, and no more heart problems. The doctor seemed a little perplexed, though. Ruby shows no signs of the brain injury or heart issues, whatsoever, from the accident, except the cuts and bruises on her face." He paused and his shoulders slumped. "But she lost her baby." He glanced back at Donald. "How is Reed?"

Donald stumbled back a couple of steps and said, "What? Ruby was pregnant? We didn't know…"

Harry's eyes began to water and he shook his head. "I'm so sorry. I thought you knew."

Donald walked over to the large window overlooking the hospital's garden and held onto the ledge for support. "I'm so sorry, for all of us."

Harry placed his hand on Donald's shoulder. "Do you think Reed knows?" They heard voices and glanced back to see two people walking down the hall.

Donald shoved his hands in his pockets. "I don't think Reed knows about the baby. He would have told us. He's up and he wants to see her. Do you think you could help us out?"

Harry replied, "They're moving her to Reed's floor. As soon as she is settled, I'll come to Reed's room. Did you know they're engaged?"

Donald removed his hands from his pockets and his eyes met Harry's. "Yes, the ring was my mother's. Reed asked for it a couple of days ago. I suppose you hadn't heard about the engagement before the accident."

Harry shook his head no. "We didn't know. Ruby's crazy about your son. Let's go back upstairs and tell Reed she's being moved." They walked over to the elevators and the doors opened. Harry and Donald stepped inside and Harry pushed the button to the fourth floor.

REED WAS SITTING ON HIS bed when his father and Mr. Glenn came into his room. Reed could tell by the sad looks on their faces something had happened and his spine tightened and it felt as though a shard of glass pierced his side.

"She's dead?" Reed held his breath for a reply. He searched their faces for answers.

Donald said, "No, Reed, she is fine. They're moving Ruby up here to your floor."

Reed wiped tears from his eyes as he sighed with relief. He asked anxiously, "When do I get to see her?"

Mr. Glenn reached in his pocket and handed Reed the engagement ring. "The nurse gave this to me. You may want to place it back on her finger when you see her." He placed his hand on Reed's shoulder and gave him a pat.

Reed held the ring in his hand and lifted his head to meet Mr. Glenn's eyes. "We were going to tell you. I love your daughter. I love her so much."

Mr. Glenn gave him a nod and said, "Let me go see if she has a room. I'll be back soon." Mr. Glenn walked to Reed's door. He glanced back at Reed and then closed the door behind him.

REED PUT ON HIS SWEATPANTS and a MTSU sweatshirt and then slipped on his tennis shoes. He sat nervously on his bed, waiting for Mr. Glenn's return, thoughts racing through his mind. Reed had planned an entirely different life for himself. He had intended to find a job with a marketing firm in Nashville, stay a few years, and then move to New York or Los Angeles to a larger agency. Travel the world, working with advertisers from Japan, China and Europe. He wanted vacations in the south of France or the countryside towns of Italy.

Then he met Ruby, and everything changed. He loved Ruby's laugh. When something was really funny and made her laugh, she would throw her head back and hold onto her sides. He knew the taste of her mouth and the feel of her skin next to his. He saw beyond her beauty to her inner self, which few others knew. Nothing in his life would ever be the same because he had her in his life. Without her, he would be lost.

Donald smiled and sat on the bed beside him. "I remember having the same look about your mother when I knew she was the one I wanted to spend my life with. Parents want their children to know true love and happiness. It doesn't mean life will all be peaches and cream, son. On the contrary, loving someone so much and then finding out they're suffering makes you acutely tuned into their pain, their suffering. More often, you feel helpless. But true love is worth it. True love is what makes life worth living. You and Ruby will move past the accident."

Reed's shoulders slumped as he turned to face his father and said, "I was mad at Ruby for being at Brent's cabin. I was jealous. I had asked her to marry me, but I was still so mad at her. That's why I was driving so fast. The wreck happened because of me." Donald circled his arm around Reed's waist. He dropped his head to his father's shoulder.

Donald took a deep breath and leaned his head next to his son's. "Well, son, sometimes love makes us do stupid things. Believe me when I say—this will not be the only time you get jealous or mad. Next time, try and think through your feelings before you act on them."

There was a quiet knock on the door and Harry walked back into the room. Reed noticed that Harry's demeanor had improved considerably in the last thirty minutes. He offered Reed a warm grin and said, "Ruby is in room 423, only four doors down, Reed, and she is chomping at the bit to see you, too. Do you need any help?"

Reed drew in a deep breath and stood. His ribs were sore, but he could walk on his own two feet. "No, sir, I think I can manage. I have a girl to go see, if you guys will excuse me." Reed made it slowly out the door and walked down the hall corridor until he saw Ruby's room number. He entered without knocking and glanced nervously around her room.

Ruby's face was black and blue with bruises, but she no longer had any IVs or monitors hooked up to her. She sat up in her bed and her eyes were bright with excitement when she saw Reed. She threw off her covers and got out of the bed. "Reed, oh, Reed, I'm so glad you're here." She hugged him and he winced in pain and Ruby quickly dropped her arms. "Oh, I'm so sorry."

He bent over and kissed her. Reed let out a sigh. "Now, I'm all better. I've been so worried about you. Tell me what the doctor said. I see the bruises, but are you hurt anywhere else?"

Lee stood up. "I think I'll take a walk, stretch my legs a bit, and give y'all some privacy. I'll put the no visitors sign on the door. I'll be back in a little while." Lee walked over to Reed and kissed him on the cheek. "You need anything?"

Reed looked down at Lee and said, "No, ma'am." He watched her leave the room, closing the door behind her.

Ruby sat on the bed and motioned him to sit down beside her. "I'm going to give you a rundown, but I need you to listen with an open mind, okay?"

Reed sat on the bed and held her hand. His eyes never lost contact with hers as Ruby relayed the whole story from the discovery in the cave, her dreams, Anna's healing powers and Sandy's abilities to read thoughts. She told him that Anna had healed her in the ICU. Ruby paused for a minute and then told him about losing Alisa and the time she had spent with their child during her stay at the in-between. Ruby told Reed about meeting Seneca in her dreams—and the choice she had made to return to him.

Reed stared at her in shock and bewilderment. He reached his hand out and placed it on Ruby's abdomen. They had lost their child. He would have slain thousands of dragons to save Alisa, but now, he just sat there helpless, not knowing what to say or how to react to Ruby's news. His thumb brushed over her knuckles, and he felt her tremble. "Will you be able to have more children?"

Her lip quivered a little before she replied, "The doctor said he didn't see any reason why I couldn't have more children."

She shifted in the bed to sit cross-legged and then grabbed his hands. "Anna healed me, Reed. Do you believe me? Do you believe what I just told you? I had to tell you about Seneca, me and the girls, if we are to have a life together. These abilities we were given have a purpose. We're just not sure what kind of purpose yet. But I believe our gifts are to help others. I didn't even know I would be able to tell you about it. There have been times in the past when I've tried to talk to my mom, and the words just vanished. The only people who know about Seneca are the girls and you."

Reed was trying to wrap his head around everything she had told him. He had the insane urge to laugh or scream. The memory of seeing her die in the ambulance still chilled his blood. She had died. His princess had died. He shook his head. This wasn't a movie, damn it, this was his life. Ruby was telling him about a mystical messenger named Seneca, and that he was real. He wanted to believe, and he had to place faith in her, to have a life with her. "Ruby, the one thing I know for certain is I love you. I have faith in you. I believe in you."

Reed lifted her hand and slipped the engagement ring back on her finger. He reached over and kissed her on the lips. "Let's get married now. I don't want to waste another minute of my life without you by my side. I will stand by you and give you what is within my power to support you. What do you think?"

Ruby gazed into his eyes and he gave her a sideways grin. She said, "I think, I have to get out of here and get a wedding dress."

Chapter 13

Show Me The Way

THE DEN AT EVERGLADE FARMS was cozy, with its fireplace and cedar bookshelves lined with books from the family's collection. The dark red leather couch had been in the den most of Ruby's life. The leather had softened over the years. Her dad's big cherry desk sat in the corner, so he could look out the window when he worked on his bills. Harry sat in his recliner every night reading the paper. The den was her father's domain.

Ruby sat in her dad's chair, looking out the front window for Reed to pull up in her driveway. Reed's dad had helped him buy a new El Camino truck to replace his totaled car from the accident. Ruby jumped up when she saw him drive up and started to run for the door, when she heard her mom yell, "Ruby Jane, don't run in the house." Ruby chuckled and bolted out the door.

She jogged down the steps and along the sidewalk to the back of the house. Max came running up beside her.

Reed got out of his car and opened his arms wide. "I have missed you warming my bed, woman. Let's go get this over with so I can take you home with me."

"I'm so ready to go. My mom, bless her heart, is driving me crazy."

Ruby and Reed entered the kitchen. Ruby looked over to her parents and then said, "Dad and Mom, we would like to talk to you."

Ruby's dad's head shot up, but then he looked back down, longingly, at his sandwich. "Now, or do I have time to eat?" Her mom walked over and playfully smacked him on the head with the newspaper.

"Honey, you and Reed sit down and talk to us. Dad can eat and listen at the same time." Lee sat down at the table and Harry joined her, his sandwich in hand.

Reed sat down with Ruby, and then he stood up again. "Mr. and Mrs. Glenn, Ruby and I want to get married."

Harry chuckled and took a bite of his sandwich. Lee frowned at him and turned to Reed. "We thought, with the engagement ring, y'all had already decided that."

Reed was nervous. He sat back down again and grabbed Ruby's hand. "Yes, we have, but we want to get married next week."

Harry choked on his sandwich and Lee smacked him on the back and handed him his glass of tea. Harry said, "Next week? We were thinking maybe y'all would wait until you graduate, Reed."

Reed rested his forearms on the table. "Well, sir, I don't want to wait another second. After the accident, I agonized over nearly losing Ruby and we did lose our child. I tried to get Ruby to elope with me, but she wants her family and friends there."

Ruby's grandfather had walked into the kitchen while they were talking to her parents. He looked at Reed and said, "I don't blame you, Reed. Seize the day. I wish you both a life of much joy and happiness."

Ruby stood up and walked over to kiss her grandfather on the cheek. "Thank you, Granddaddy."

Lee poured everyone a glass of sweet tea and topped off Harry's and then sat at the table. "I see the love you two have for each other, there's no denying it. I'm so happy for you both. It's okay with me, if it's okay with Harry."

Harry took the last bite of his sandwich and wiped his mouth with a napkin. He took a drink of tea and set down his glass. "I have a compromise, if you two will hear me out. I realize you are both adults now. Your mother and I can't stop you. But if you will wait until the semester is over, then we will help you both, until Ruby can graduate." He walked over to the calendar, pulled it off the kitchen wall, and placed it on the table.

Harry flipped the calendar to the month of December. "Here, Saturday, December tenth. Sounds like a good day to get married to me. The house will be decorated for Christmas. That's a little less than two months for y'all to set up house. There's a lot more to being married than smooches, Cricket."

Ruby's face turned bright red. She walked over to Reed and sat down beside him. "Reed, will December tenth be okay?" Ruby looked up into Reed's eyes and he nodded yes. "I'm going to still live in the Bell Street house until Reed and I find a house."

Harry chuckled. "Baby girl, we'll help you any way we can. Okay, Mama?" Lee nodded okay, and Harry said, "Well, Reed, what do you say?"

Reed circled his arm around Ruby's shoulder. "That sounds like a plan to me."

Ruby thought about getting married in the family room in front of the fireplace with the Christmas tree and all the trimmings. She kissed Reed and then turned to her parents. "December tenth sounds like a fine day for a wedding. I want to get married here. We don't want a big wedding. It will be so much more fun with just the Glenns and Jacksons and our close friends."

Lee eyes were shining with enthusiasm. "Sounds great to me! We'll have so much fun getting ready for the big day. Since you're out of school the next couple of days, how about us girls taking a road trip to Nashville for dresses?"

Harry grunted. "Oh lord, I hear my wallet wailing now."

Reed walked over to shake Mr. Glenn's hand and Ruby's daddy gave him a bear hug.

"You're part of the family, son. Get used to hugs and kisses; we Glenns are in limitless supply."

The family laughed at Harry's comment. Ruby hugged her parents. "I have a few things upstairs in my room I want to take into town." She grabbed Reed's hand. "Would you help me?"

Reed stood up. "Yes, ma'am."

As they walked off, Harry said, "Boy, it's just starting. You'll be peppered with "honey do's" the rest of your life."

Chapter 14

Dancing In The Moonlight

RUBY LOOKED AT HER REFLECTION in the mirror. She had found an elegant but simple wedding dress. Ruby's wedding dress was a winter white with a shirred, strapless bodice, a sweetheart neckline and a floor-length skirt. The silky dress fit her like a glove.

Anna and Sandy had come over early to help her get ready. Anna smoothed Ruby's hair after she had secured the veil in place. "Any dreams last night?"

Ruby gave her friends a smile and then replied, "Nope, Seneca has been pretty quiet since the accident. Maybe he's giving me a break. What about you guys?"

Anna stepped back and placed her hands on her hips. "Nothing since the wreck."

Sandy shrugged. "Me, neither. We'll get together when you get back from your honeymoon and go over any new entries to our Ditch Lane Diaries. Right now, Ms. Glenn, you focus on your wedding day and your wedding night." Sandy's brows wriggled up and down. Anna and Ruby both laughed.

Anna looped her arm in Sandy's and said, "Ruby, you're divine in that pretty spectacular dress. Reed's gonna pass out when he sees you."

Sandy held onto Anna's arm and gave Ruby a once-over. "You'll do, and let's pray Reed doesn't pass out. See ya downstairs, girlfriend." Sandy laughed and dropped her arm away from Anna and reached over to give Ruby an air kiss to the cheek. Anna followed suit and they left Ruby's bedroom.

Ruby walked over to the window, looked out at their Tennessee farm, and reminisced. She had crammed in a lifetime of experiences and memories over the last six months. There was a knock at her bedroom door.

Ruby opened the door and her dad said, "Cricket, are you ready?" He had big tears in his eyes. "My precious baby girl, you look so beautiful today."

Ruby reached up and kissed her dad on the cheek. "Thank you, Dad, for everything."

He took a deep breath and smiled as he hugged her. "Well then, I believe they're playing your song. May I?"

Harry took her hand and placed it in the crook of his arm. Ruby grabbed her flowers and they made their way down the stairs. At the entry to the great room, everyone stood and turned to face them. George's friends played a beautiful rendition of "The Wedding March" on acoustic guitars. The room was lit by the warm glow of candles, twinkling Christmas lights, and the fireplace.

The only way Ruby could describe the feeling in the room was it was similar to the first day she met Reed: electric. And Reed, well, he was simply the handsomest groom she had ever seen. Reed wore a dark navy blue suit with a white dress shirt and a pink tie. She giggled. Ruby had bought him the pink silk tie. He had laughed at the color but had told her he loved it anyway. He stood so proudly, waiting for her, with love in his eyes. Reed took her breath away.

REED WATCHED AS RUBY ENTERED the great room. She was the love of his life. Her red-gold hair fell over her shoulders under a veil of antique white lace. Her dress flowed around her. She had a dreamy, soft look in her eyes as he met her gaze. Reed could barely contain his emotions from the love he felt for Ruby.

Reed was sure when he looked back, years from now, at this precious moment, he would remember her beautiful face, her sweet smile, and the tears that trailed down her cheeks when he held her hands.

Pastor Logan began the ceremony. "Who gives this bride to this groom in marriage?"

Harry said, "Her mother and I do."

Ruby's dad took her right hand and placed it in Reed's left hand, and then Harry walked over and sat beside Ruby's mother.

The pastor continued, "Reed and Ruby come today desiring to be united in Holy Matrimony."

Pastor Logan offered a simple prayer to bless the couple, now, and in the years to come. He opened his eyes and smiled first at Reed and then to Ruby. "I ask you each now to repeat the marriage vows."

Reed started: "I, Reed Harley Jackson, take you, Ruby Jane Glenn, for my wedded wife. To love and cherish, for better or worse, for richer or poorer, in sickness and in health, until death us do part."

Ruby was nervous and began to giggle, which made Reed chuckle silently. She could hear Max barking wildly outside the window.

"I, Ruby Jane Glenn, take you, Reed Harley Jackson, for my wedded husband. To love and cherish, for better or worse, richer or poorer, in sickness and in health, until death us do part."

The pastor then asked for the rings and said, "Bless, O Lord, the giving of these rings, that they who wear them may live in your peace and your favor all the days of their lives. Through Jesus, our Lord. Amen."

Reed placed the ring on Ruby's finger and said, "This ring is my sacred gift to you, a symbol of my love, a sign that from this day forward, my love will surround you. With this ring, I thee wed."

Ruby placed the ring on Reed's finger and repeated the same words to him.

Then the pastor announced, "For as much as Reed and Ruby have consented together in holy matrimony, I now, by the authority committed unto me as a minister, declare Reed and Ruby are husband and wife, according to the ordinance of God. In the name of the Father, and of the Son, and of the Holy Spirit. Those whom God has joined together, let no man put asunder."

The pastor grinned broadly and said, "Now, Reed, you may kiss your bride."

Reed dipped Ruby backward and kissed her so passionately she momentarily forgot people were watching—until she heard Georgie whistle loudly.

They turned to face their family and friends and the pastor declared, "Allow me to present, Mr. and Mrs. Reed Jackson."

Everyone started yelling and clapping and Ruby's mom was crying. Jerry was in the back of the room and popped the cork of a champagne bottle. The Jacksons had brought buckets of the bubbly. Anna and Sandy began handing out glasses of champagne to everyone.

There was a flurry of excitement as everyone congratulated the newly married couple. George's friends continued playing music. The wedding party moved into the dining room, which had been decorated with silver and white Christmas décor. The dinner was marvelously romantic, and by the time everyone had his or her chance to say a toast, their bellies were full and Ruby was more than slightly intoxicated.

Reed kept kissing her and stroking her cheek or pressing his leg into hers. When it was time to cut the wedding cake they moved the party back to the great room where the photographer captured the moment when Reed and Ruby joined hands and cut the first piece on a table which had been set up next to the bar.

Jerry and George moved the chairs from the wedding out of the way to allow for a makeshift dance floor. They staged the stereo, and once the cake festivities ended, the dance music began to play. Reed escorted Ruby to the floor for their first dance as husband and wife.

As they danced Reed whispered in her ear, "Your silky wedding gown reveals every sweet inch of your all-too-enticing body, honey."

A blush lit her cheeks as heat washed over her. "You're a bad boy, Reed Jackson, but God, I love you!" He let out a low growl, sending a shiver up her spine, and she pulled him to her and kissed him passionately. She heard whistles and catcalls behind them.

Neighbors and friends stopped by to congratulate the happy couple and joined in the party. The party was so much fun and the house was full of people. It would be one of the most precious memories of Ruby's life.

The time passed by so quickly. Her wedding day, her vows, and the celebration seemed to flash by her in an instant, and then Reed was there, scooping her up in his arms.

Reed said, "It's time, princess. Are you ready?"

Ruby held his hand and their fingers linked. "Always."

Reed and Ruby had already changed clothes upstairs and now joined their parents at the door to the front porch. Ruby and Reed's embrace fell away so they could give hugs and kisses to their parents. Then they ran for his truck, while their family and friends threw birdseed mix, instead of rice. Ruby hoped there weren't any bats that got funny ideas. The guys had decorated Reed's truck and the girls had made a "Just Married" sign and placed it in the back windshield. Ruby rolled down the window and waved as they drove down the driveway and onward to the Nashville Airport.

Epilogue

Simple Twist of Fate

RUBY HAD LIFE OR DEATH dreams. Her life dreams foretold the birth of a child and her death dreams saw the passing of a loved one, and occasionally her dreams gave her glimpses into the future. Ruby had had those dreams since she had entered the cave and found the hidden room, the totem and the stones. Today, she worked behind the counter at Everglade General Store. There had been a steady stream of customers all day.

Ruby was keeping an eye on the customers in the back of the store when the front door bell chimed and she looked up to see two of her regulars walk in. She organized the items next to the cash register and sprayed the top of the counter, wiping it down before the next customers came up to check out.

The two customers in the back of the store walked up to the check-out register. While she rang up their sales, she listened to the banter back and forth between the two. Ruby looked up to see Mr. Burns in his office, rising to walk out into the store.

Ruby placed her hands on the counter and leaned toward the two customers. A playful smile lit her face, as she looked from one, to the other. "Y'all need to stop this right now and grow the freak up. I'm not going to play your little dating game." She looked at Reed, whose mouth hung open, and said, "I will meet you at Ditch Lane in exactly one hour. Do not go anywhere, okay?"

Reed looked back at her rather perplexed and nodded okay. Then she turned to Brent, pointing her finger at him. "And you, I will never go out with you." Ruby heard Reed laugh loudly, as she continued, "But I do have someone in mind for you who would be just perfect."

Reed looking rather stupefied asked her, "Uh, ah—how did you know?"

Ruby grinned and said, "I can see the future." Reed lifted his brow and gave her his sexy sideways grin and her stomach flipped.

Reed looked over to Brent, who opened his mouth to say something and then closed it again. Reed slung his arm over Brent's shoulder, grabbed their drinks, turned and walked out the store doors. Before stepping outside, Reed glanced back at her and grinned, then left the store.

Ruby's regular customers were in line to check out. Ruby smiled at little Tommy's mother. She looked down at Tommy and placed her hands on her hips. "So, Tommy, I see Mr. Burns has finally given you the toy fan."

RUBY PULLED INTO DITCH LANE with the single-minded purpose of finding Reed. As she passed her friends, they tried to talk to her, but she didn't stop—she continued toward Reed without breaking her stride. She spotted Reed talking to her brother, George. Reed's head shot up when he saw her walking swiftly toward him. Reed moved a step away from George. His eyes locked with Ruby's gaze. The energy building between the two of them rapidly increased, sending embers from the bonfire flames flying upward to the sky.

Ruby's circle of friends stood near the bonfire: Anna, Sandy, George, Lizzie, Jerry and Brent. Ruby tossed a quick glance to Sandy and Anna who had turned to watch her, but she ignored their stares as she increased the speed of her step. She came only a few feet away from Reed, as recognition lit his eyes and a sideways grin curved his lips. Ruby ran and jumped up on Reed, locking her legs around his waist, cradling his face with her hands and covering his mouth with hers in a mind-bending, soul-binding kiss. Reed turned them slowly around in a circle as their kiss deepened and lengthened, and he held on to her even tighter. She loved him and never wanted to let him go.

George chuckled. "*Ruby Jane*, I didn't know you even knew Reed."

Anna and Sandy laughed and clinked their beers in a toast. Anna bit back her laughter and shouted to the sky, "Dy-no-mite!" Anna turned Jerry to catch his hand, but he had turned and walked away from the crowd, so Anna dashed after him.

Brent leaned over to Sandy and asked, "So, do you have a boyfriend?"

Sandy's eyes met George's and held for an instant and he turned away to Lizzie. "I don't do the boyfriend thing. But I do date…"

Ruby's mind was spinning from her dream's revelation that Reed Jackson was her lifelong love and her only choice. From the time Ruby had entered the cave's hidden room, she had had dreams about her relationship with Reed and she knew him the moment he entered the store.

Ruby had met the mystical messenger, whose image had been carved into the cave wall, in her dreams. His name was Seneca. What Ruby mistook as astronaut's headgear the day she had seen his image in the cave was Seneca's radiance, all about him. The ancients had merely tried to capture Seneca's aura in their drawings.

Seneca had given Ruby, Anna, and Sandy gifts. Ruby—the dreamer, Anna—the healer, and Sandy—the soul reader. Ruby's dreams would take her to meet Seneca and they would enter a room filled with pure gold, as clear and as transparent as glass, and she would walk to a floor to ceiling crimson curtain. Seneca would allow her to enter behind the curtain and Ruby would see the future, the dreams had played in her mind like vivid feature length films. He gave her the choice to intervene on behalf of the friend or loved one.

Ruby had intervened for her Aunt Sammie. The day her aunt should have died, Ruby convinced her aunt to go hiking the backwoods of Campbell Ridge with her. Ruby saved her life. Ruby had decided not to intervene in Cathy's life, her friend from high school. Ruby's dream gave her the details of Cathy's cheating husband, but she knew Becky, her daughter, would be the best part of Cathy's life. Ruby had remained silent.

Seneca revealed in her dreams about Anna and Sandy's gifts and how all three of them were to use their gifts for the greater good of mankind. The girls would be facing major challenges over the years and evil would be coming for them. Ruby would tell Anna and Sandy about her dreams, at the assigned time designated by Seneca, when they moved into the Bell Street house. The girls would create the Ditch Lane Diaries that would give them direction to their path. As they matured, so would their abilities.

When Ruby intervened on behalf of someone, there were consequences that created ripples in time, changing people's lives forever. She would pray for guidance when making those choices.

Ruby's dreams revealed parts of her future, but trying to navigate her choices about her own future had been tricky. In her dreams, she had seen Reed and Brent and what would have happened had she not intervened tonight. Reed was her destiny. She had made the right choice.

SIX MONTHS LATER, ON DECEMBER tenth, Ruby and Reed were married at Everglade Farms.

The Ditch Lane Diaries

Ruby's Choice is the first book in the Ditch Lane Diaries. *Anna's Way*, the second book in the series, is currently underway. Look for *Antique Mirror*, a short by D.F. Jones coming fall of 2015. Register for updates online at www.dfjonesauthor.com.

Happy reading!

About the Author

Here's a little information about me. I grew up in Middle Tennessee. Unlike Ruby's idyllic childhood, mine was a little rocky. I nearly lost my mother in the sixth grade to a terrible car accident. She was in and out of the hospital for several years. Writing became a part of my life. I used writing as a form of therapy. I wrote poems and plays. I started my own school newspaper. My beautiful mom did eventually recover, and she continues to be an inspiration to me today.

I graduated from Middle Tennessee State University with a Bachelor of Science degree and landed a job with the ABC affiliate in Nashville. I started writing creatively for my clients, and eventually opened my own media company.

After years of writing creative for other people, I decided to write something for myself. It turned into my debut novel, *Ruby's Choice*. If you love to read and get immersed into the characters of a book, then you will catch a small drift of how incredible it is to write your own characters and breathe them into life. I love every second of writing, well, maybe not the snip, snip of some scenes. But, even cutting scenes, you begin to see the novel take shape. It's a wonderful feeling, and I applaud every author who has had the tenacity to see their project through to the end. I love *Ruby's Choice* and I trust you will enjoy reading her story.

All the best!

D.F. Jones

Made in the USA
Lexington, KY
30 July 2015